A Christmas Homecoming

Sunriver Dreams Series
A Love to Treasure
A Christmas Homecoming

A Christmas Homecoming

SUNRIVER DREAMS BOOK TWO

By Kimberly Rose Johnson

ACKNOWLEDGMENTS

I would like to thank my beta readers, Janice, Tina, and Sherry for their insightful input. You ladies rock! I would also like to thank my editor Kathryn Davis for her suggestions as well. Without all of you this story would not be what it is.

Thank you!

CHAPTER ONE

BAILEY CALDERWOOD PULLED THE KNIT HAT her mother had given her last Christmas lower on her head as freezing wind whipped her long hair, tossing it into her face. Wind whistled between the tall ponderosa pines that surrounded her employer's house near Sunriver, Oregon.

Why had she agreed to move to Mona Belafonte's home? On a good day her employer was difficult to please, but now that she'd had a stroke, most of the time she was impossible. Not that Bailey blamed the woman for being difficult. She had to be frustrated and angry at her situation and slow recovery.

Bailey needed to take care of her task quickly and get back to the house. Mona didn't like to be alone. Thankfully the youngest of the Belafonte brothers was returning from France next week in time for the holidays. From what she'd been told, he worked with the design side of the business as well as the construction side, and she was hoping having him here would brighten Mona's mood and speed her recovery. The task of freshening his cabin should go fast. But since it had been closed up for the past two-and-a-half-years, there'd probably be a good deal of dust to contend with.

Crunching metal and shattering glass punctuated the early afternoon air. Bailey's stomach clenched, and her pulse jumped. *Oh no!* The noise had come from the direction of the road. Snow nipped at her ankles as she jogged along the driveway that wove through the woods to the road.

A small pickup with steam rising from under the crumpled hood had wrapped around a huge pine. The driver slumped behind the wheel. She bounded through the snow and yanked open the door. Blood streamed down the man's face. She fought rising panic. What if he was dead? She nudged the man's shoulder, noting his expensive suit and tie. "Sir, wake up." *Please be alive.*

"Don't." He pushed at her. "Leave . . . me . . . alone." His head rolled to the side.

She yanked her hand away. Was he drunk? She sniffed but didn't smell alcohol. What should she do? She'd left her cell phone at the house. He may not want her help, but he definitely needed it. She patted his face. "Hey, wake up. We need to get you out of here."

No response.

Maybe if she shook him—no. What if he had a head injury? She bit down on her bottom lip. A glance at the steaming hood caused her panic to rise.

She didn't think the pickup would catch fire, but she'd seen enough vehicle explosions on TV to prompt fear. He was too large for her to get him out on her own. She needed him conscious. *What do I do, Lord?* Looking around for anything that could help, her gaze rested on the snow. It was worth a try.

She balled clean snow in her hands and applied it to his head. The cold ought to wake him, and it would help with the nasty gash too.

A minute later, he groaned and slowly his lids opened. "What happened?"

Maybe he had a brain injury.

"You crashed. Other than the gash on your head, are you okay?" She wanted to shout at him to hurry and get out but forced herself to at least appear calm. No flames were coming from the hood—yet.

He shifted and winced. "I think so, but I hurt in places I didn't know existed." He barked a laugh.

Fear gripped her. Was this man gravely hurt, or had he miraculously escaped serious injury? What if he had internal injuries? She straightened and looked around at the scene. There was no evidence of another vehicle being involved—probably a deer or a patch of black ice had caused him to lose control. At least the engine had stopped smoking or steaming or whatever it'd been doing. "I imagine you're going to be sore for a few days. By the look of your eye, I'm guessing you'll have a shiner too."

He brought his hand to his face and flinched when he made contact with the area around his eye.

"Your pickup is a mess and won't be going anywhere without a tow."

Blood oozed from the gash on his forehead. Suddenly woozy, she rested a hand on the pickup. This man needed her help, and she was the only able-bodied person around for miles. A tissue box on the floor at his feet caught her attention. "Hold on a second. We need to get you out of here, but first . . ." she slid her arm beneath his legs and grabbed a wad of tissues, then pressed them to his forehead. "We should stop this bleeding."

He jerked away. "Hey!"

"I'm sorry. I didn't mean to hurt you."

He laid his hand over hers. "It's okay." His voice gentled. "I've got it. Thanks." He released his seatbelt and gingerly stepped out of the Ford Ranger 4x4. He swayed.

She slipped an arm around his waist. "Easy there. Don't want you falling or passing out." She chuckled nervously. "I've already got one invalid to take care of." She shot him a smile, hoping to ease the tension that hung between them.

He gave her a lopsided grin. "How is my mother doing?"

She loosened her hold on the man and looked at him more closely. He had the Belafonte blue eyes and broad shoulders. "You're Stephen?"

He nodded, then gasped.

Her insides knotted. Though obviously in pain, he put up a strong front. She admired his strength. Maybe keeping things casual would help get his mind off his discomfort. "We weren't expecting you until next week. Your mom will be thrilled to see you." She shot him a grin.

"Mother made it sound like she needed me, so I came back early. Are you her assistant?"

"Yes. I'm Bailey."

"Good to meet you. However, I wish I'd made it to the house first. Let me grab my bag." He gingerly moved away from her supporting arm.

The man, who towered over her five-foot-seven-inch frame, slowly ducked his head and reached across the seat.

He twisted back around, holding a small duffle bag. Pain etched on his face.

She pushed her glasses up higher onto her nose and stuffed her gloved hands into her jacket pockets. "Is that all you have?"

"I like to travel light."

"But you've been out of the country for a long time. How could you only have one small carry-on?" She'd heard of traveling light, but one bag was extreme.

He quirked a grin. "Sorry, I was trying to be funny. The airline lost my luggage."

"Figures. You're really having a bad day."

"I've had worse." A haunted look darkened his eyes as he limped along the snow-covered driveway toward the house.

Her heart tripped. From what she'd been told, he had experienced much worse. She matched his slower pace. "I'm sure

Mona will be thrilled that you came home early. Should I take you to the hospital? Or would you like to come to the main house and let me bandage the cut on your head, and wait and see how you feel?"

"I'm fine. Let's go to the house. I'm anxious to see my mother."

Stephen glanced at the woman beside him, still trying to understand what his mother had been complaining about in her emails. Bailey seemed pleasant enough, even sweet. Her tender concern for him touched him deeply. It'd been a long time since someone showed that kind of care toward him.

Mom tended to get caught up in appearances so that was probably where Bailey failed. Her attire didn't meet his mother's standards. The red and hot pink knit cap on her long, kinky hair looked homemade, and the too large jacket she wore over her jeans didn't do her any favors. His teeth chattered. If he didn't pick up the pace, they'd both end up with hypothermia. He lengthened his stride even though every step hurt. He should have thought to have his brother, John, leave an extra pair of boots in his pickup. At least then, he wouldn't have soaking cold feet. No one besides John knew he was coming home a week early. His brother had been a huge help by dropping his pickup off at the airport. He still couldn't believe Mom had had a stroke.

He glanced toward Bailey and caught her watching him closely. Compassion lingered in her hazel eyes. She pushed her large, dark-rimmed glasses higher on her nose and shot him a look of concern—or was it unease? "Are you okay?"

"I was wondering the same thing about you." She rested a

hand on his arm. "You're injured, just totaled your pickup, and I'm not sure, but you probably have a concussion. Who knows what else is wrong—and you're worried about *me*? At least let me carry your duffle bag."

He started to shake his head then thought better of it. What he needed was a hot shower, a painkiller, and an espresso. "Thanks for the offer, but I've got it. So tell me, how is my mother really doing?"

"Are you sure you want to hear this right now? It's not good."

"Positive." The worried look in her eyes unnerved him. Were things worse than he'd been told?

"Okay, but if you want me to stop, please say so."

"You're kind of freaking me out. Please tell me."

"Sorry. I suppose she's doing as well as can be expected, but she's not a young woman, and from what I understand, her road to recovery will be long. She can't be alone for any length of time because she has anxiety attacks, which has made keeping the business running smoothly a challenge. I can't do the job I'm being paid to do and take care of your mother. Sooner or later our clients are going to start complaining. I'm an interior designer, not a nurse, or a good cook or housekeeper." She pressed her lips together and looked away.

"What's wrong?"

"I said too much."

"Yet, I sense there's more." He stopped and waited for her to look at him. He gave her the look that usually made grown men squirm. "I appreciate that you are being brutally honest with me, and even though I don't know you and my head is pounding, I insist you tell me what you left out."

"Okay, but for the record, dumping this all on you right now may be more than you want to hear."

"I'll take my chances," he said drily. Bailey had spunk. He liked that.

She crossed her arms. "I'm really worried about her. I take her to therapy sessions, and she doesn't seem to be improving. On top of that, she was diagnosed with type 2 diabetes, and she refuses to eat right. Granted, I'm not used to cooking for a diabetic, and I've been struggling with how to feed her, but she is such a picky eater. It's been a challenge."

"I hadn't heard about her diabetes." Worry gripped him. Mom tended to be a drama queen, so keeping something big like that quiet must mean her health was far worse than she'd let on.

"She's a private woman, so I'm not surprised."

"Seriously? My mother loves attention."

"Not all attention is desirable."

"True." He still remembered the looks of pity he'd received after his wife died. Their pity was one reason he'd fled to France.

"I doubt anyone besides her doctor and I know. Unfortunately, her mood has been less than happy, and she doesn't want to be told what she can and can't eat. I'm at a loss for how to help her." She snapped her mouth closed.

"I see." Although the diagnosis surprised him it shouldn't, since the disease ran in the family, but why hadn't Mom told his brothers? Surely one of them would have hired a cook for her. "I wish someone had told me the extent of her problem. Had I realized how bad things were, I would've come home as soon as I learned of her stroke. I'm sorry you've been dealing with this on your own. I take it my family has been of little help?"

"They do the best they can."

What was going on here? It wasn't like his brothers to neglect family. Stephen's stomach knotted. If his mom was doing so poorly, why hadn't anyone told him, and why was an employee of their construction and design company taking care of her and not family? What had happened to everyone while he was away? "Thank you for being honest. Now that I'm here, your responsibilities will shift to your actual job. My mom has always been tight with money and refused to hire out for work she can do herself. Considering the circumstances, though, maybe I can talk her into allowing me to hire a cook. But I make no promises. She is a stubborn woman."

Bailey nodded. "Are you planning to stay in the main house?"

"No, but I will spend several hours each day there so you can slip out and deal with your actual job."

The worry in her eyes made him wonder, but right now he'd talked all he could. The house came into view, and he stopped. The snow set off the mountain-like lodge as if welcoming him home. "Wow, it still looks amazing."

She chuckled. "I'd have thought you'd be immune to its beauty."

"Never," he breathed softly and continued forward. Decorative greenery and pinecones hung from the cedar pillars that supported the wrap-around porch, giving it a festive feel. "Nice touch. Did you do that?" He motioned with his free hand toward the porch.

She nodded. "I started decorating last week. Mona plans to host Thanksgiving and Christmas here and wants everything to be perfect."

"I thought she was stuck in bed."

"Not anymore." She shrugged. "I guess she's improved, but not as much as I'd hoped. She gets around, but slowly and with the help of a walker. Some tasks are harder than others for her."

Bailey led the way up the porch steps and pushed into the house. "There's a first aid kit in the kitchen. Take a seat, and I'll be right back." She scurried from the massive entryway and disappeared around the corner.

He settled into the nearest chair. Nothing had changed in the two-and-a-half years he'd been gone. It even smelled the same—like vanilla. Not even the furniture had been moved, or the picture of him and his late wife Rebecca that rested on the mantle. He swallowed the lump in his throat and averted his eyes.

"Here we go." Bailey popped the top off the kit and tore the wrapper off an alcohol swab. "This will probably sting."

He sucked in a sharp breath—she wasn't kidding. "How bad is it?" He studied her face for a hint at the condition of his wound. Her hazel eyes with speckles of gold gave nothing away.

"It's actually not nearly as bad as I expected, considering how much it bled."

Her tender touch didn't surprise him. Bailey had an air of gentleness about her—she radiated quiet. No wonder Mother was going nuts. She liked constant action and noise. Rebecca and Mother had gotten on very well. She was like the daughter Mom never had. Those two together had been a force of nature. He chuckled.

"Something funny?" A beautiful smile lit Bailey's face. Her eyes sparkled in the dancing light from the picture windows.

"Being here brings back memories."

"Good ones I hope." She applied a couple of bandages to his forehead.

A whisper of pine scent wafted the air around her. She must have been working with the branches before she'd discovered his wreck. Her leg brushed against his.

"Mostly." Awareness shot through him. He reached up and gently grasped her wrist, drawing her hand away from his head. "Thanks. I'll take it from here."

She stepped back, slipping from his grasp. "Okay. If you start to feel like you need to go to the hospital, let me know."

He started to tell her he could take care of himself, but the concern in her eyes stopped him. "Thank you."

"Will you be okay for a bit by yourself with your mom? There's something I need to do."

"Sure."

She still wore her outdoor clothes, and her tennis shoes were squeaking as she stepped past him toward the door.

"You should wear boots."

She turned to face him. "Excuse me?"

"Your shoes are soaked. Your feet will get frostbite."

She looked down. "I don't have far to go." She spun around and bolted from the house.

Surely, she wasn't embarrassed by his comment. But something sent her fleeing.

"Bailey!" His mother's clear voice drifted down from upstairs.

He'd nearly forgotten about her. He rushed up the sweeping staircase as quickly as his sore muscles would allow and burst into his mother's bedroom.

She sat up in her bed. "Oh!" Mom's eyes filled with sudden tears that quickly streamed down her aging cheeks. "You're home." Her words came out slowly, but clearly.

He sidled up to her bed. "I am."

She wiped her eyes with a shaky hand. "You look awful. What happened?"

He could say the same about her but knew better than to comment about the side of her face that drooped slightly. Mom had always hidden her age well, but her seventy-three years were evident now. "I hit a patch of ice and wrapped my pickup around that old Ponderosa Pine I wanted you to let me take out years ago. That thing is a menace." He quirked a grin to make sure she knew he was teasing.

She wrapped his hand in hers and gave it a weak squeeze. "I'm glad you lived to tell me about it. Now, where's my addle-brained assistant? I don't know what's gotten into her lately. Ever since she moved into the house, she hasn't been herself." Her brow furrowed as she looked past him toward the door.

He'd only met Bailey a short time ago, but addle-brained didn't fit his impression of her at all. More than likely Mom's demands were frustrating the poor woman. "Perhaps you are expecting too much of one person, Mom." She'd always been a taskmaster. Dad had been a good balance to her Type A personality.

"Nonsense. I pay her well to do her job. She should rise to the occasion." She looked past him toward the doorway.

"Bailey went outside to take care of something, but I'm all yours. What do you need?"

"A time machine."

"Come again?" Had the stroke given her brain damage too?

"I'd like to rewrite history. No stroke for me and no accident for you."

He grinned then grimaced as pain pulsed in his face. At least she hadn't lost her sense of humor.

"Since you are so quick to defend my assistant, what did you think of her?"

"She's fine." He liked her quite a bit actually, which surprised him considering his mother's attitude. It's not like they'd be spending much, if any time together—although now that he'd met Bailey he wouldn't mind.

"Mm-hmm, but what's your impression of her?"

Were they really going to have this conversation now? With a sigh, he sat on the edge of the bed. "She came to my aid at my pickup and patched me up." He pointed to his forehead. "She's a bit reserved, but she's kind." He shrugged. "We only met a little bit ago." He remembered her gentle touch as she cleaned his wound and grinned.

Mom harrumphed and crossed her arms. "Since you don't seem overly impressed by her, I want you to start searching for a new assistant for me immediately."

"What? I don't think that's a good idea." Alarm shot through him.

She narrowed her eyes. "I'm still running this business. Don't forget that."

This was not a good time to be hiring someone new with the holidays so close. Bailey seemed competent and was certain to know the ins and outs of the business. It would be difficult to train someone new. Granted he'd only met Bailey, but his defenses rose for the young woman nonetheless. After all, she'd rescued him from his accident. Then again, if his mother wanted her gone, he should honor her wishes. He'd have to tread carefully with this situation.

CHAPTER TWO

Bailey breathed in a sigh of relief to be away from the main house and Stephen. The man had an effect on her she didn't care for—a cross between nervousness and awe. He was a Belafonte and therefore her employer. She needed to keep her distance. They were from two different worlds, and she would never fit into his. She'd put that nervous energy to good use cleaning his cabin.

She flipped on the lights in Stephen's cabin and turned full circle from her position in the center of the main room. The cabin, though nothing in comparison to Mona's palatial home, was perfect to her way of thinking. A river rock fireplace occupied the wall directly across from the entry with an urban-rustic coffee table placed between it and a brown leather couch. A room-sized rug with soft brown and blue tones covered the floor between the couch and the fireplace. Occasional chairs balanced out the space.

She held a swag of holly leaves and berries mixed with small pine branches that she'd brought over earlier and left on the front porch. Perhaps hanging it on the door outside would be best. Now that Stephen was home, it felt wrong to be in his home without his knowledge or permission. But Mona would want the place freshened and welcoming before he moved back in, so she needed to hurry and ignore her unease.

After hanging the decoration, she reentered the house and pulled open the closet, hoping to find cleaning supplies. "At least one thing is going right today." She quickly brushed a feather duster against the light fixtures, then dampened a cloth and wiped dust from all the solid surfaces.

She finished dusting and stood still for a moment deciding what to do next. The uncluttered place really only needed a quick run-through with the vacuum. She plugged in the appliance, which instantly whirred to life, and puffed a cloud of dust into the room.

"Oh no!" She jerked her head to the side searching for the off button when the vacuum suddenly shut down.

"What are you doing?" Stephen stood in the doorway with crossed arms, his bag on the floor beside him.

"I . . . well . . . I was supposed to be cleaning, but I'm afraid I made things worse."

"Being my housekeeper falls under your job description?" He raised a brow and closed the door behind him.

"No. But your mother asked me to tidy up for you."

He carefully wound the cord and placed it on the hook on the backside of the upright vacuum. "I should have thrown this thing out years ago, but Rebecca thought it could be fixed." A look of pain crossed his face as he wheeled it to the door.

Bailey clasped her hands together. His slumped shoulders ignited something inside her. "I don't mind cleaning. I was hoping to finish this and be gone before you came over."

He turned, weariness clouding his face. "Don't worry about my home, Bailey. Regardless of what my mother says, cleaning my cabin is not your job." He pulled the front door open and stood to the side, meeting her gaze. "I'm jetlagged and in desperate need of sleep."

What she saw knotted her stomach. He pitied her! She raised her chin, and heat rushed through her body as she marched past him. She turned before leaving. "Welcome home. I hope your injuries heal quickly, and if you need anything, you know where to find me. Sleep well." She kept her voice calm in spite of the irritation that bubbled to the surface. She closed the door and trudged along the path through the woods toward Mona's.

A silver car sat in the circular driveway in front of the house. Relief washed over her. She wouldn't need to deal with Mona now that the Certified Nurse's Assistant was finally here—an hour late, but at least she was here. They'd arranged to have a woman come in once a day for a few hours, so Bailey could meet with clients. Now she could head into Sunriver and finish the house they'd been hired to redecorate. The delivery truck would arrive in forty-five minutes. Barely enough time to stop in at Nicole's home for a cup of coffee, but she wouldn't stand up her friend.

A quick dash to her bedroom for her purse and computer, and she was off. At the end of the driveway, the sight of Stephen's totaled pickup made her ease up on the gas. Not that she was going fast, but a little caution would be wise.

A short time later, she pulled up to Nicole's house. She was later than she'd expected.

Nicole stood in the doorway. "Everything okay? I thought you'd be here an hour ago. I sent you a text, but you didn't reply."

Bailey rushed to the door. "I'm so sorry I'm late. This day did not go at all like I'd planned."

"I can tell. What has you so out of sorts?" She stood at the kitchen counter and poured coffee into two mugs.

Bailey grinned. "Thanks." She brought the coffee to her nose and sniffed. "What kind is it?"

"A pumpkin spice mix."

"Yum." She sat at the kitchen table and took a sip. Tension eased from her shoulders. She needed this. "I should buy a bag. Mona would love it too."

Nicole added cream to her coffee. "You look like you were in a battle and lost. I thought you had a job to go to after this."

Bailey's hand shot to her hair. "I do. Stephen had an accident and then the vacuum exploded all over me. I was so rattled I didn't think to look in the mirror." She ran a hand through her hair. "I must be a mess, and I'm supposed to meet clients in thirty minutes."

Nicole leaned in. "Hold on a second. Who is Stephen?"

"Mona's son who's been in France." She fingered a napkin that lay on the table and tore it into tiny bits as she told her friend about Stephen and his accident. "And now I'm totally out of sorts and off schedule." And apparently a mess too. But nothing could be done now. She had to keep her appointment or Mona would ax her for sure.

"You could've canceled. I would've understood."

"Not a chance. I needed to see a friendly face."

Nicole stood and grabbed her cup. "Come on. You can shower here before your appointment. You're covered in dust. Be sure to wash your hair too. I'll fix it for you when you're done."

"I don't have time for all of that. I'll just wash my arms and face off."

Nicole shook her head. "Trust me on this." She pressed her lips together, grabbed Bailey's arm, and pulled her into the master suite. "I'm sure there's something in my closet that will work since we're close in size."

Bailey's insides leapt. "You're a lifesaver, but I need to hurry. I can't be more than twenty minutes late."

"Don't worry, make the call and get moving. Everything you'll need is in the bathroom." She pulled a robe from the closet. "This is brand new. Put it on when you get out."

"Okay. Thanks." Bailey took the robe, made the call, then raced into the bathroom she'd played a large role in remodeling over a year ago. When she turned the space into a luxurious spa she never imagined she'd one day get to use it.

She looked in the mirror and gasped. Dust on her dark, frizzy hair made her hair look gray, and a smudge of dirt on her nose finished the ragamuffin look. Her hair could use a deep conditioning for sure to get her tight curls under control. No wonder Stephen pitied her. She was a mess! Good thing she'd called Mrs. Gladstone to warn her she'd be late.

Her client would have been scandalized by her appearance. Bailey quickly hopped into the shower and washed the dust out of her hair then ran shampoo and conditioner through her hair, hoping to tame the frizz. Five minutes later she slipped into Nicole's thick, white spa-like bathrobe and padded into the bedroom.

Her friend held a black A-line skirt and a long sleeve red sweater. "What do you think?"

"Perfect. Thank you."

Nicole frowned. "Not perfect. Your sneakers won't go with this, and we don't wear the same size shoe."

"I keep black boots in my trunk."

"You change while I grab them, then I'll do your hair." Nicole scurried from the room.

Ten minutes later, after she had donned the skirt and sweater, Nicole pulled her hair into a French twist. "I can't thank you enough, but I have to run."

"Go. We'll catch up another time. Before I forget, what are you doing for Thanksgiving?"

"Mona asked me to cook, so I guess I'll be with them." She hoped she could pull off the meal.

"Mark invited Spencer, and Sarah will be here. I'd love to have you come too if anything changes."

"Okay, thanks. Wish me luck."

"You don't need luck, but I'll pray. I put your clothes into a bag and set it by the door."

"Got it. Thanks again." She fingered the bag and raced to her car. The house she was going to was only a few minutes up the road so she'd only be ten minutes late. She almost wished she hadn't agreed to spend Thanksgiving at the Belafontes', but she wasn't one to back out of commitments. She'd love to spend the holiday with Nicole and her fiancé Mark. Sarah was really nice too. She didn't know Spencer, Mark's friend on the Sunriver police force, as well as she knew the others, but he was a nice enough man.

A short time later, she pulled up to the client's home. A delivery van took up the driveway. Was that Mona's Buick parked beside it? She frowned and set the brake. There was no way Mona would be here.

The door to the home swung open, and Stephen walked out holding a clipboard. "Glad you made it. I had everything moved into the garage and checked the invoice. It looks like it's all here."

"Sorry I was delayed." Why was he here? Wasn't he supposed to be sleeping?

The homeowner peered around Stephen's arm. "Bailey! You look lovely."

Stephen looked up, and his eyes widened.

"Thank you, Mrs. Gladstone." Bailey hoisted her purse onto her shoulder and stepped up the stairs. No one had ever told her she looked lovely—especially a high-and-mighty kind of person like her client. She breezed past Stephen, catching a whiff of his Obsession cologne. "Shall we get to work?" Her heart kicked into double time, as if it could beat any faster. What was Stephen doing here? He should be at home resting.

Stephen held back the grin that threatened to escape. He hadn't intended to throw Bailey off, but it became clear the moment shock registered on her face he should have called to let her know Mona demanded he supervise. Well, maybe she didn't need to know that part. He didn't want to offend her. After all, she had come to his aid after his accident, plus he was depending on her to do her job.

She cleaned up well. Who would have thought such a beauty was hiding behind the messy state he'd seen her in earlier. No wonder Mother hired her. She was beautiful in an understated kind of way.

Thoughts of his mom unsettled him. He had no idea what had come over her. She used to be such a fun loving person, but the CNA informed him that Mom was normally grouchy. She had always leaned toward temperamental; perhaps her health issues were getting the best of her. Whatever the problem, he was here to make sure everyone stayed happy. Even if that meant putting his wishes aside for a short time.

He followed after the women to the great room. Bailey had a layout of the room pulled up on her laptop. Good. This shouldn't take too long. He was sore and jetlagged, and his body said it was well past time to be in bed. He imagined it would take a few days to adjust to Pacific Time.

Bailey raised her chin. "Mrs. Gladstone, I hate to kick you out, but I would love to surprise you with the finished room in two hours—maybe less."

The older woman plastered on a stiff smile. "Okay. I will be upstairs if you need me, but I'll be back in exactly two hours." She plodded up the stairs and disappeared out of sight.

Bailey whirled around, worry etched in her face. "Where's my muscle? Bob and Jacob were supposed to meet me here."

"Rick needed them at the jobsite in Bend." His oldest brother had called the house a short time ago, and since he was going to be on site anyway, it wasn't a problem. "That's what I'm here for. Together, we can get everything in place." Plus working with Bailey would give him a chance to better assess her on the job skills.

She looked at him as if he'd lost his mind. "Good thing I told her two hours. We'll need it."

He squared his shoulders. "Is there a problem?" Did she doubt his strength? Maybe he hadn't been to the gym in a week or two, but he could get the job done.

"Sorry, but you're injured, and by your own admission, exhausted. And I'm not exactly a powerhouse of muscle." She flexed her arm.

He held in a chuckle but couldn't stop from grinning. She was cute when she was annoyed, but enough playing around. "I'm all you have. I suggest we get busy. You only gave us two hours."

She pressed her lips together. "You're right. We'll bring in the rug and then the furniture, followed by accessories." Her boots clicked across the hardwood flooring.

He turned to look over his shoulder. Pain shot through his neck. He gasped.

"You okay?"

"I'm sorer than I realized, but don't worry. I can help."

"I'm counting on it, but you should take it easy as much as possible. I'll feel bad if you injure yourself further." She stepped around him and pulled open the door leading to the three-car garage. "There's more stuff than I remembered. Hopefully two hours is long enough."

"We'll get it done." The worry etched on her face made him all the more determined to complete this project in less time than allotted, even if he did want to sleep for the next month.

They went to work. He had to hand it to Bailey. She worked hard and fast. She knew exactly where everything should be placed and when something didn't look like she'd imagined, she quickly adjusted. The woman had talent.

Two hours later, he hung the last picture, and a gasp broke the silence as their client strolled down the stairs. "It's perfect!" She ran her hand across the 1940s antique bar cabinet Bailey had said she found on eBay. "I see why you wanted this to be a surprise. The mix of old with new is perfect." She reached for Bailey's hand. "Thank you. I will be sure to let Mona know how pleased I am."

"You're most welcome and thanks. Anytime you want to redecorate, I hope you'll give us a call."

"I will." Mrs. Gladstone walked them to the door. She turned to Stephen. "Please tell your mother I hope she feels better soon."

"Will do." He dipped his chin and followed Bailey out to her car. "Great job in there. She really liked what you did. My mom said this was your first solo job from start to finish."

Bailey's eyes sparkled behind her dark-rimmed glasses. "Yes. I've given a lot of input on other projects and even took over various aspects, but this is the first time I was given the freedom to take a project from concept to fruition. I couldn't be more pleased with the outcome."

"I'm glad." And he was. It was almost as if she stood an inch taller after hearing Mrs. Gladstone's praise. "I should probably head home. The CNA agreed to prepare extra meals for my mom, but I don't want to take advantage of her time. She said something about wanting me to taste test the meals before freezing them." He'd expressed his concern about his mother's eating habits, and she'd seemed very anxious to help.

"Must be your good looks because she refused to stay longer to cook when I asked for help." She hopped into her car and slammed the door.

Now that she mentioned it, maybe the nurse assistant *had* been flirting with him, but it hadn't occurred to him until Bailey's comment. He shook off the thought and slid into his mother's car. What was he going to do about Bailey? His mother's demand that he find and hire a replacement ate at him. He liked his mom's assistant. She lightened the mood in a room, even when she was being serious. Obviously the woman had talent, so what was the problem? And could he fix it before his mother took matters into her own hands?

CHAPTER THREE

A WEEK LATER BAILEY PULLED OFF her glasses and rubbed her aching eyes. At this rate she'd never find the style of dresser their client demanded. Why did everyone want vintage lately? Buying new would be so much simpler.

"Bailey!" Mona called from the room next door.

"I'll be right there." She tried to keep her voice cheerful, but it was becoming more of a challenge. With a click on the mouse, she closed the internet and put her computer to sleep, suspecting this would take a while. Grabbing a notepad and pen she ambled into her boss's bedroom. "Oh." A tingle zipped through her as she stopped mid-step. *Get it together girl.* No way would a man like Stephen give her more than a passing glance. She needed to turn off this attraction before her heart got involved. "Hi, Stephen. I didn't realize you were here." The black eye he'd gotten from his accident last week had turned colors and was now an odd shade of yellow.

"Good afternoon, Bailey," Stephen said. "Mrs. Gladstone called a while ago. She was still ecstatic over the job you did for her and told Mother how pleased she was with your work."

Bailey grinned as she walked to the empty wingback chair on the other side of Mona's four-poster bed. "Thanks for letting me know. I'm really pleased she liked it so much."

"Well, that's the point of hiring a professional," Mona snapped from her bed.

The euphoria of a moment ago fizzled. Her boss sure knew

how to make herself understood. It seemed her speech had improved slightly since Stephen's arrival. Then again, Mona was still talking slower than normal.

"If she wasn't happy, there'd be a problem." Mona crossed her arms.

Stephen cleared his throat. "That's true, Mom, but I believe when a job is well done it should be acknowledged."

Bailey's gaze shot to Stephen's. He winked. Stephen was different from his brothers. None of them ever winked—period. She had imagined Stephen would be stuffy and disagreeable, considering that he'd chosen to work in France—a location decidedly more aristocratic than Central Oregon. Plus, he'd gone there on his own; it wasn't even the family business he was working for. Maybe she'd judged him wrong. His shortness with her last week could easily be attributed to his accident and jetlag.

Stephen cleared his throat. "My mother and I have decided to hire a companion for her. Someone who will fix meals, keep the house tidy, and tend to her needs. I hope to have her in place soon after Thanksgiving. Then maybe Mom will be more willing to venture outside this room."

Bailey's gaze shot to Mona's. Her boss frowned, but a resigned look filled her eyes. "I think that's a wonderful idea." In fact it was the best news she'd received since Mona's stroke. Not that she didn't feel for her boss, but life would be so much easier with help. She had to believe that if Mona would get out of that bed and try a little harder to gain back her mobility, her overall health would improve.

Mona pressed her lips into a tight frown.

Bailey's eye's widened. *Uh-oh.* Mona was unhappy, and that never bode well for anyone. Clearly her son had played a huge role in getting his mother to agree to hire someone. Hopefully she'd warm up to the idea and turn that frown upside down, as her mom liked to say. Bailey had never thought of using an old fashioned companion who could do it all. He'd found the perfect solution.

Mona's hurtful words from a moment ago tickled the back of her mind, but she pushed them aside. She would not dwell on words spoken out of anger, frustration, or perhaps pain. She did a good job and would keep this job by continuing to be excellent at designing and pleasing their clients. "What can I do for you, Mona?" Her boss had called her in here for a reason, but they'd gotten sidetracked.

"I want to go over the design for the Davis's en-suite remodel. Rick wants the plans firmed up so they can begin work on Monday."

"Okay. It's on my computer. I'll be right back." She placed the pad and pen on the chair and dashed to the next room to retrieve her laptop. A moment later she settled in the wingback again and pulled up the file. "I've already received approval from the homeowner and planned to send this over to Rick today." She passed her computer to Mona.

Mona raised a brow. She scrolled down and nodded. "This is fine. Thank you."

Bailey grinned. "If there's nothing else you need from me, I'll get back to work."

"How are the plans for our Thanksgiving feast coming along? Do you have the decorations?" Mona asked.

"Yes. Everything will be exactly as you requested on Thanksgiving." That was, almost everything. She'd much rather be with friends or family, but if Mona needed her to make this holiday special, she'd do it. The Belafontes were a decent bunch—at least most of the time—and she adored Rick's children, Lacy and Collin. She'd spent a good deal of time with the kids, since as Mona's assistant, retrieving her grandchildren from school and entertaining them fit into her job description. She was glad that Mona now trusted her with creating and implementing designs. After all, that was the reason she'd sought the job.

"Good." Mona passed back the computer and closed her eyes. "I think I'll take a nap."

Stephen stood. "Okay, Mother. Rest well." He followed Bailey from the room, closing the door behind them. "I'm really sorry about Mom. I believe her condition is getting on her nerves, and you appear to be her kicking post."

Her heart warmed toward this man, who was turning out to be nothing like she expected. "Thank you, Stephen. There's no need to apologize for her, though. She's a grown woman and responsible for her own behavior. I appreciate you talking her into hiring a companion. It's a better idea than getting a cook, and I believe the help will free up my time so I can do my job."

"That's the plan. And you won't need to worry about the companion at all. My mother and I will train her. She'll occupy the room across the hall from Mom's."

"Sounds great. Well, I should get back to work." She spun around and marched downstairs to the office. The phone rang, and she raced to grab it. "Belafonte Designs, Bailey speaking."

"Bailey, I need you down at the site pronto. We have a problem," Rick, the oldest Belafonte brother said.

"Okay. Care to give me a hint?"

"It's best if you see for yourself."

Concern gripped her. It wasn't like Rick to overreact about things, so this must be serious. "I'm on my way." She grabbed what she needed and raced for the door. She'd been to the site of the new house last week and everything had been running smoothly. What had gone wrong? The last thing she needed was a major problem when she had so little time to spare.

"What's the rush?" Stephen asked from his position at the

window facing the front of the house.

"Rick needs me at the site." She didn't have time to explain nor did she want to. Without waiting for a reply, she darted to her car and prayed for safety. She really disliked driving in snow, and a fresh coating covered the road.

Once on US 97 she noticed a silver car behind her. Was it the same vehicle that had been tailgating her on Century Drive? She moved into the right lane. Why didn't the driver pass her? The car moved behind her. Unease gripped her. Why was this person so intent on staying close to her?

The highway had been cleared of snow, so she increased her speed. The silver car kept pace with her. Her chest pounded, and the car suddenly felt too warm. She cracked a window and kept going. Maybe if she slowed he would also. Several cars whizzed by, but not the silver one.

What should she do? Maybe he wasn't really following her. Maybe he was simply following by coincidence. That had to be it. She signaled and made a right. The silver car did too. Fear like she'd never known before gripped her. The probability of that driver heading to someplace on this street was low. The build site loomed ahead. Several trucks were parked out in front. All she had to do was pull up behind one of them, grab her purse, then race inside. The elevation here was quite a bit lower than Sunriver, so there was no ice or snow on the ground to impede her.

Without signaling, she braked hard, slammed the gear to park and bolted inside. She peeked through the window, but the silver car was gone. *Whew!* Okay, so maybe she'd overreacted. It wasn't like there were no other homes on this road, but still the likelihood of that driver coming from Sunriver to here was slim.

Her pulse slowed, and she realized her hands shook. She needed to get a grip before Rick noticed and thought she'd lost it. Speaking of Rick, he stood at his truck talking on his cell phone wearing a grim look. She took a bracing breath, went back outside, and approached him.

He pocketed his phone. "Thanks for getting here so quickly. Is everything okay? You pulled in pretty fast. I called out to you, but I guess you didn't hear."

She shook her head. "Sorry. I was distracted. What's the emergency?"

"You need to see this."

She followed him into the kitchen and gasped. "What happened?" Graffiti covered the custom walnut cabinets. "How?"

"We had the place secured, but whoever did this busted in the back door. Thankfully the cabinets for the rest of the house weren't installed yet. What do you want to do?"

"Can we order new ones?"

He shook his head. "No time. It would take months to get them. We can do stock cabinets. I know the owners want to move in as soon as possible."

"We'll need to clean these up. Sand and re-stain them. Let's get the custom cabinet company in here to clean these up, unless you'd rather do it yourself. The homeowner was very specific about what she wanted."

"I'll contact them today. Sorry to bother you with this."

"It's fine. I'm glad it wasn't something worse. You had me scared. As long as I'm here, I'll check the overall progress." She was in no rush to leave. Her nerves were shot after the drive here.

Rick trailed her through the place, taking notes as she pointed out things that still needed attention. "How's it going with my mom and Stephen?"

She glanced in his direction before climbing the stairs to the second level. "Fine. Your brother seems to be settling in, and your mom is mostly the same." She stopped mid-step. "Mona is getting a personal companion to see to her needs, including cooking her meals and housekeeping. Isn't that great?"

"I'll say! We should have done that to begin with."

"Agreed." She continued through the house.

"Never thought I'd see the day when Steve would come back, but I guess he can't hide from the past forever."

She shot him a look over her shoulder. "His past?" She knew Stephen's wife had died, but was there more?

"He was a mess after Rebecca died. When the opportunity to leave the country came, he snagged it so fast he left us in his dust."

Bailey strolled into the guest bath at the top of the stairs—the plumbing still needed to be installed. It looked like they were a little behind schedule, but in this case it was a good thing, since the vandals hadn't been able to ruin anything in here. She turned to face Rick. "Your brother sounds like he went through a rough patch."

Rick snorted. "I suppose you could call it that. Are we good on everything here?"

"Yes." They talked shop a little longer, then the conversation shifted. "I'm going to stop by the bakery before I head back to Sunriver. What are your family's favorite kind of pie for Thanksgiving?"

"Pecan, chocolate cream, and pumpkin. The chocolate is for the kids."

"Perfect. I'll order one of each. Anything else I should plan to have on the menu?" She'd never been in charge of a holiday meal and having to prepare one for the boss's family was more than a little daunting. What if it was a disaster?

Rick picked up a scrap piece of wood and pulled a squarish shaped pencil from his tool belt. He wrote on the wood, then handed it to her. "Make sure the meal includes all of those things and you're golden. I'll catch you later, Bailey." He strode down the stairs.

She stared at the list. Turkey, dressing, mashed potatoes, cranberry relish, and homemade dinner rolls. She'd order the rolls from the bakery, along with the pies. Hopefully they'd taste homemade enough.

"Bailey?"

She turned at the sound of Judy's voice. Rick's wife didn't usually come to the job sites. "This is a surprise."

"I'll bet." Judy raised her chin and narrowed her eyes. "I was about to say the same to you. What are you doing here?"

"Rick needed me for something." Unease gripped her. What was up with Judy? She looked ready to attack. "I need to order pies for Thanksgiving. I'll see you Thursday."

"Right. You sure that's the only reason you're here?" Judy asked.

"I think so. There was some vandalism, and Rick had a design question. Oh, and to get a list of the kind of pies your family likes."

Judy smiled, but it didn't reach her eyes. "Aren't you the sweetest? You'd better get a move on if you're going to get the order placed. I came to visit my husband."

"Okay then. See you." Bailey went outside. A knot formed in her stomach. Judy seemed to be suggesting she was up to no good, but that didn't make sense. They'd always gotten along fine.

Bailey looked around for the silver car and breathed a little easier when she couldn't find it. She was being paranoid and probably imagined the tension with Judy. Sunshine made her squint, and she wished she'd remembered her sunglasses. At least the sun had decided to come out. She'd missed it the past few days. A car parked across the street grabbed her attention. She shielded her eyes and a tingle shot through her. What was Stephen doing here?

He stepped out and waved. "Glad I caught you." He strode

over to her.

"What's up? I ran into Judy a moment ago, too."

He frowned. "Really? I didn't think she liked to come around the job sites. She's always said they're too dusty and dirty."

So that's why she'd never seen the woman visiting her husband before. What had changed? Why had she come today? "Hmm. I hope everything is okay."

He frowned. "You think something's wrong?"

"I didn't say that. But it is strange that she'd be here."

"I agree. I'll ask my brother about it later."

"Why not ask Judy?"

"We've never been close, and somehow I don't think she'd appreciate me questioning her."

His explanation made sense. Judy wasn't the friendliest woman. "What brings you here?"

"I wanted to see what Rick's working on. Plus . . ." He pulled a piece of paper from his pocket "My Mom asked me to make sure you got this." He held it out to her.

"What is it?" She took the paper he handed her.

"A recipe for cranberry relish." He looked at her with uncertainty on his face. "I know my mom can be demanding, but I hope you don't mind using her recipe."

"Not at all. Thanks for bringing it by. It's helpful. I should be going. I have several stops to make before I head back to Sunriver." She hesitated. "Who's with Mona?"

"No one. Why?"

"You left her alone?" Her voice hitched. "She can't be alone, Stephen. What if she has a problem, or the house catches fire, or any other number of things? She's weak from getting very little exercise."

"She can walk, can't she?"

Bailey nodded. "Technically, yes, but not well and not far. I thought you understood your mother's situation."

"Apparently not well enough. I'd hoped to visit with my brother and take care of a few things while I was out, but I'll go back there right now. Run your errands." Sincerity filled his eyes. "I'm sorry about this. It won't happen again."

She nodded, more than a little surprised he was willing to alter his plans. Then again, Mona was his mother, and she thought the world of him. He must pamper her, because Mona only adored people who catered to her.

Bailey left the house more curious than ever about the youngest Belafonte brother. There was so much she didn't know about Stephen, but one thing she did know—sadness seemed to surround him. She wanted to help, but there was only so much she could do. Mona was her top priority, at least until they found a companion. She probably shouldn't worry about either of them, since she had a strong feeling Mona was trying to find her replacement and using Stephen to help her, but she couldn't help herself.

She frowned as she pulled into the grocery store parking lot. In spite of whatever was going on behind the scenes, she refused to disappoint the Belafonte children. Rick's kids were sweet, and for them, she'd stick it out and do her best to prepare a fantastic Thanksgiving meal.

CHAPTER FOUR

EARLY THANKSGIVING MORNING, BAILEY STOOD AT the mirror in her bedroom and pulled her hair into a ponytail. The house was still quiet and peaceful, exactly the way she liked it. Hopefully Mona would sleep a couple more hours. It would be nice to hide out in the kitchen for a while uninterrupted. Once she had the turkey in the oven, she'd feel a lot better.

She needed a cup of coffee and a muffin to settle her nervous stomach. Her mother would reprimand her for drinking coffee instead of tea when her stomach was a bundle of nerves, but Mom didn't understand that the scent of coffee was calming for her.

She'd be sure to give her parents a call while she ate breakfast. Giving herself a once over in the mirror, she frowned. Her dark wash jeans and new purple, cashmere blend sweater were a gift from her mom. She wanted to look nice today but didn't want to ruin her new clothes while cooking, either. Oh well, she'd throw an apron over it and call it good.

She slipped into her most comfortable black boots, then headed downstairs. Soft Christmas music greeted her as she entered the kitchen. Stephen stood bent over, sliding something into the oven. "Good morning."

He straightened. "Hi. I learned to cook in France. I hope you don't mind that I prepared the turkey." He wiped his hands on the black apron wrapped around his waist and shot a grin her direction.

She caught her breath. *He cooks*? Why did he have to look so good, even wearing an apron? "Not at all." She spotted the box of muffins she'd picked up at the bakery on the countertop beside the fridge, exactly where she'd left it the evening before. "Would you like to join me for coffee and muffins? These muffins are so perfectly sweet, you'd think you were eating dessert."

His brow furrowed. "Isn't it a little early for that?"

"Nope." She pulled it from the counter and raised the lid on the box. "Jenna makes the best melt-in-your-mouth cinnamon streusel muffins I've ever had. I bought three. One for each of us, and I make a great pot of coffee. I get my beans from Brewed Awakenings in Sunriver, in case you want to get some for your place." She'd set the timer on the coffee machine the night before, and it suddenly clicked into brew mode. Good, she was more than ready for a caffeine fix.

Although she'd looked forward to a quiet time visiting with her parents on the phone, spending a little time with Stephen was a good idea too. She sensed he could be a good ally where Mona was concerned.

"Sure, why not. If you can't have dessert for breakfast on Thanksgiving, then when can you?"

"Right." She placed two white mugs on the counter and filled them with the rich brew, then grabbed the box and sat at the island. "How are you feeling? Any lingering effects from your accident?"

"I'm mostly doing better. The soreness is about gone, and as you can see, my eye is almost healed."

She noted the bruise had pretty much faded. "So what are your plans for the day?"

"Mom's nurse will be here in about an hour to help her get cleaned up and ready for the festivities today. Once she leaves, I guess I'm on Mom duty since I haven't found a suitable companion for her yet."

"You've only been looking for a couple of weeks. The right person will turn up." Bailey added creamer to her coffee and drew in a deep breath, savoring the rich scent. "Mmm." She grinned and imagined what it would be like to begin every day like this. Especially considering all she had to do today. "Mona seems happier now that you're here. I'm sure it will help her improve." Although as feisty as ever, her boss had softened since Stephen's arrival, and anything that put Mona in a good mood, Bailey supported.

"Really? I think she's been somewhat cantankerous."

Bailey chuckled. "That's her normal demeanor. But I've heard that happy people get better faster."

He wrapped his hands around his coffee mug and stared at the brew. "She wasn't always like that. Sure, she was a bit on the stuffy side, but she was fun too—sarcastic and hilarious. Rebecca and my mom were quite the pair." He shook his head, and the merriment left his eyes.

"I'm sorry about your wife."

He nodded and finished his muffin and coffee in silence. "I'll check the turkey from time to time, but otherwise I'll stay out of the way." He stood and rinsed his dishes before loading them in the dishwasher. "Thanks for breakfast." He winked and strode from the room.

"Hmm." Bailey rested her elbows on the countertop and tapped her chin. Stephen was a difficult man to figure out. Was he still mourning his wife or had something else changed his demeanor? Too bad she couldn't read minds! She glanced at the wall clock and pulled her phone out. She still had time to call home. She tapped her parents' number on speed dial, and her mom answered after only two rings. "Happy Thanksgiving!"

"Bailey, it's so good to hear your voice," Mom said. "How are you?"

"A little nervous about preparing today's menu, but the hardest part has already been taken care of. Stephen, Mona's son who's been away in France, already had the turkey in the oven when I got to the kitchen this morning."

"Now that sounds like a handy man to have around. Your dad would never dream of helping in the kitchen, as you know."

"Speaking of Dad, what's he up to?"

"Chopping wood out back. I can get him for you."

"No. We can talk later. I don't want to interrupt."

"Okay. We'll miss you today."

"Thanks. What are you and Dad going to do?"

"Since our *only* child isn't here, we thought we'd go out. There's no sense making a big meal for the two of us."

"Really?" Mom had always invited friends from church or extended family over. She never dreamed her not being there would create such a change. "I'm sorry to have messed up tradition."

"Don't worry. You did me a favor. I've always wanted to let someone else do the cooking."

Bailey heard the truth in her voice, and her guilt eased. "Okay. Enjoy yourselves."

"We will. Have a lovely day, dear." Mom's voice caught.

They both finally said a teary goodbye.

With a sigh, Bailey stood and donned an apron. It shouldn't take too long to throw together finger food and side dishes. An hour later she had fruit and veggie platters sitting in the refrigerator, then began work on the cranberry relish Mona requested.

Stephen popped into the kitchen. "The nurse is with Mother now and will be for at least an hour. I thought it'd be a good time to set the table, before I head back to my place."

Bailey smacked her forehead with the palm of her hand. "I

totally forgot about the table." How could she have done that? Design was her profession.

"No worries. You've been otherwise occupied. Don't think your hard work is going unnoticed."

She stilled. "Thanks, Stephen. That's nice of you."

He chuckled. "I'm a nice guy when I'm not jetlagged and injured."

"Duly noted. I'll have time as soon as I finish this relish. I can at least help carry the dishes to the dining room."

He waved her off. "I've got this. Put your feet up when you're finished."

She added the final touches to the relish and grabbed a fork to taste test it. She forked a small amount into her mouth—not bad. Hopefully it would meet Mona's expectations. Stephen sang along to the Christmas music. He had a nice voice. Between his skills in the kitchen, his melodious voice and kind heart, it was a wonder that he hadn't been snatched up while in France. Having Stephen here was proving to be a much better thing than she'd expected.

Stephen stood with one hand on the mantle in his cabin and the other holding a picture of Rebecca. "Things here are so weird without you, Rebecca." One minute he felt as if everything was as it once had been, then the next he felt like the bachelor that he was years ago. Like when he'd winked at Bailey. He'd done it without thinking, but the look of surprise on her face was branded into his mind.

When would he be able to shake this melancholy that plagued him? He was lonely and ready to move on with his life.

He'd thought he'd done that in France, but now that he was home again, all the memories flooded his mind day and night.

Then there was his mother. He hadn't let on to Bailey how poorly Mom was doing, but Bailey was a smart woman, and he could tell she at least had an inkling. When he'd received the call that he needed to come home to help care for his mother, he didn't know what he'd expected to find here, but seeing her so frail was definitely not it.

He'd been away less than three years, and she seemed to have aged twenty. She was no longer the spry woman he remembered. What more could he do to help his mother?

He set the picture back on the mantle. For now he'd check on the turkey and see if Bailey needed any help in the kitchen. She was extremely organized, so he doubted she would, but he'd offer nonetheless.

He slipped into his jacket and boots, then stepped outside. A cold blast of air struck him. He tucked his chin and headed for the shortcut thorough the woods that led to the main house. John's Jeep sat in the driveway. Of his two brothers, he'd been closest to John before Rebecca's death, but they'd grown distant since. He hoped to remedy that soon. If being in France had taught him anything, it was that family was important.

He stomped to get the snow off his boots then stepped inside the house. Warmth immediately enveloped him. He shrugged out of his jacket and left it on the coat rack. He sniffed and grinned. The scent of roasting turkey filled the air. He looked around the first level. John must be upstairs visiting their mother.

Stephen rounded a corner then headed toward the kitchen. Bailey stood at the counter whistling a Christmas tune with a red apron covering her front. She had a counter filled with all kinds of desserts as well as finger foods. The second oven appeared to be in use, and a pot simmered on the stovetop.

Bailey turned toward him as he entered. "Hi. Your turkey sure smells wonderful. I can't wait to taste it."

"Me neither. I'm getting hungry." He used a digital thermometer to check the turkey's temperature. "It's almost done! I thought it would take a lot longer. I better call Rick and tell him to get over here."

"John is with Mona. He said to let him know when everyone got here."

"I'll take care of it. Don't worry. You've done more than enough already."

Her cheeks flushed a soft shade of pink. "I wanted everything to be perfect. This is my first Thanksgiving away from home, and the first I've ever cooked."

"And you're spending it with us? I'm sorry."

She laughed. "I like your family, Stephen. It's not a hardship." She grabbed a veggie platter in one hand and fruit platter in the other and left the kitchen.

An hour later Stephen ambled slowly beside his mom as she shuffled into the dining room with the aid of her walker right as Rick placed the turkey in the center of the table. He had to hand it to Bailey—she'd pulled off an elegant affair right down to the gourmet pies on the side buffet.

"Happy Thanksgiving, everyone," Mona said.

His entire family turned. His niece and nephew's faces lit.

Judy, Rick's wife, jumped up from her seat. "Mona, you look wonderful." She gave her a side hug. "I'll get her settled, Stephen."

"Okay." He stepped away. He'd extended the table to seat eight, but there were only seven place settings. Bailey was missing. Had she changed her mind about eating with them? It seemed unlikely, considering she'd seemed genuinely pleased to be spending the holiday with his family. "Excuse me while I find

Bailey." She had to be in the kitchen.

"She's gone." Judy helped his mother to her place at the head of the table.

"What do you mean, she's gone? She's been working in the kitchen all morning."

Mom shot him a look that said to zip it, but he was tired of her attitude toward her assistant who was more a part of his family than he'd been of late. He still hadn't discovered what had happened that caused his mother to turn on the woman she'd groomed for the past two years. Nor had he taken the time to search for her replacement. "Where did she go?"

"I phoned her a little while ago," Mom said, "and told her to take the rest of the day off once the meal was ready to serve." She flicked a pumpkin colored napkin into her lap.

Judy settled into her seat beside her daughter, Lacy, wearing a smug look. "She said something about meeting friends in Sunriver."

"Oh." Why did Judy look so pleased that Bailey had left? Irritation threatened to dampen his good mood. He was thankful Bailey had friends she could spend the meal with, but felt badly that she'd thought she was eating here and then was sent away.

He pulled out a high-backed wooden chair and sat next to his nephew, Collin. Bailey probably preferred to spend the holiday with friends or her own family rather than co-workers, anyway. But regardless, the arrangement didn't sit right with him. She'd been talking all week about what she was planning to make and looked forward to tasting the pies from a bakery that was supposed to be the best in the area. She'd looked forward to the turkey, too.

Mom's face glowed even though it still showed the effects of the stroke. "I'm delighted to have all my family under one roof after so long." She shot a look of approval toward Stephen.

"Welcome home, Son. We've missed you."

Stephen nodded.

"I'm thankful for each of you. I am a blessed woman and can now die happy."

He resisted rolling his eyes. Mom could be so melodramatic. "You're not allowed to die yet."

"I'm not a young woman. You never know."

John, his middle brother, cleared his throat. "Seventy-three isn't that old."

"No way!" Collin's eyes widened. "Grandma, you're way older than my Sunday school teacher, but she has gray hair. How come you don't?"

Stephen chuckled and patted his nephew's shoulder. "Cool it, dude."

Judy's face reddened, and her eyes shot daggers at her son. "Everyone is old to a seven-year-old."

"True enough," John said. "Let's pray and eat before everything gets cold."

They all paused while Rick prayed a blessing over the food. "Amen."

A low hum filled the room as food was passed and plates were filled.

"How is the search coming along for my new assistant?" Mom asked.

Rick started choking. His wife patted his back. "What are you talking about? Did Bailey give notice she's leaving?" He looked between Mom and Stephen. "The way you've been treating her, it wouldn't surprise me," he mumbled under his breath loud enough for everyone to hear.

"Let's not discuss business." Stephen shot his brother a look intended to silence him. "It's my first holiday home in a while, and I'd like it to be pleasant." Or at least as pleasant as possible.

Mona shrugged. "I don't know what the big deal is." She added fruit salad to her plate. "Thanks for bringing this, Judy. It wouldn't be a holiday without it."

Stephen tuned out the conversation around him and pondered what was going on with his family. They were all the same, yet different. Then again, maybe he was the one who had changed. Losing Rebecca made him realize what was important and what wasn't. Death had a way of doing that.

John told a joke that had everyone laughing. He'd missed it but grinned anyway. Coming back had been the right thing. Now all he had to do was figure out how to live here without Rebecca.

"I saw on the internet that Mount Bachelor has enough snow to open the inner tube run today," John said. "Anyone want to go after we eat? It's not every year they're open on Thanksgiving, so this is a treat." John looked directly at him.

"Um, sure. I guess." Stephen reached for his water goblet.

"It's settled then. The old fogies will stay here and clean up, and you, the kids, and I will go have fun," John said.

Collin pushed his plate toward the center of the table. "I'm done!"

Everyone laughed.

His niece, always the reserved one, whispered into her mother's ear. "Lacy wants to know if she can invite Bailey." A sour look covered Judy's face for a moment, then quickly cleared.

Stephen stilled. What was up with that? "She's with friends."

Lacy pushed the mashed potatoes around on her plate. "I know, but she's so much fun to play with."

"You play with Grandma's assistant?" Somehow this news didn't surprise him, but it should have.

Judy sent a forced smile his direction. "I work fulltime now, and sometimes Bailey gets the kids from school. No big deal. It's not like she's not getting paid."

"Is there anything that woman doesn't do for this family?" He shoved back his chair.

"I don't know what you're so upset about," Judy said. "Bailey is always willing to do whatever any one of us wants. It's not like we force her."

Judy appeared clueless to how callous she sounded. "Excuse me. I have a call to make." He stood and stalked out the door. He couldn't explain why this latest news didn't sit well, but he was beginning to believe his mother's words. Bailey did whatever his mother demanded and more. She was too nice a person to be treated so poorly, and he intended to put a stop to it.

Bailey, Nicole, her fiancé, Mark, Spencer, and Sarah, a close friend of Nicole's, were all seated around Nicole's dining room table. Contentment settled over Bailey. She'd felt sad at first to be excluded from the Belafontes' Thanksgiving feast since she'd worked in the hot kitchen all morning to create a fabulous meal for the family, but her backup plan turned out to be as good or better.

Her friend hadn't cooked, but they'd enjoyed a delicious store-bought turkey meal. Although Nicole didn't enjoy cooking, she'd made an effort to create a homey atmosphere, and Bailey appreciated the cornucopia centerpiece overflowing with dried flowers and ornamental gourds.

Bailey's phone rang from her purse on the couch in the living room. She looked at her friends. "I'm sorry. I forgot to silence my phone. I can't imagine who'd be calling me *today*."

"It's probably your parents," Nicole said. "Didn't you say you didn't get to talk with your dad earlier? You should answer it. Go ahead and talk in the guestroom."

"You're sure?" Bailey hated disturbing everyone's meal.

"Yes!" Mark and Nicole chimed in at the same time.

Bailey pushed back and bolted for her phone. The caller ID showed Stephen. Her heart leapt. She rushed into the bedroom and closed the door. "Is something wrong, Stephen?"

"No. Yes."

She chuckled, but unease filled her. "Which is it?" She sat on the edge of the queen-sized bed. "Was something wrong with the food? Or is it your mother?" Her heart beat a rapid staccato. As difficult as Mona was, she didn't wish anything bad on her.

"My mom is her usual self. The food was delicious thanks to you, but I want to make one thing clear. You are only my mom's assistant. Nothing more. Nothing less."

She jerked her head away from the phone as if she'd been struck. Sudden tears pricked her eyes.

"From now on you will not cook, clean, play nanny, or whatever else my crazy family has you doing. Understand?"

Her face heated. Where did he get off calling her and chewing her out on Thanksgiving of all days? "I don't understand why you are so bothered. As your mother's assistant I *assist* her however she needs help. Read my contract. And until you hire a companion for her, who else is going to do those things? You? I have to go." She disconnected the call and powered off her phone. Her hands shook. She'd never spoken to anyone like that. Her mother was right when she used to tell her that she was a grump and lacked a filter when she was tired. What had she done?

A soft knock startled her. "Come in."

Nicole slipped inside. "You okay?"

"You heard?"

She nodded. "The walls are thin."

Bailey clasped her hands in front of her to still the shaking.

"I don't know how I feel, but I hope I have a job to go back to on Monday. I hung up on my boss's son. The worst part about all this is that I can't avoid him until then, since I'm living at Mona's house right now." She hated confrontation, but it appeared she'd walked right into it without even realizing it.

Nicole frowned. "Hmm. That doesn't sound good."

"It's not. For some reason, Stephen doesn't like that I do things for his family outside of what he considers my job description. I don't know why it bothers him so much, but he made it abundantly clear he wants me to stop."

"It sounds like he's being protective of you. He cares. It's actually kind of sweet. Like your knight in shining armor."

Bailey stilled. Could Nicole be right? He was kind to her, but she doubted very much his motivation was overprotectiveness.

"What are you going to do?"

Bailey shrugged. "If I still have a job, I'll keep doing what I always do. I like being employed, and Mona has taught me a lot. I don't mind helping her with things that are not directly related to the company. The Belafontes need all the help they can get right now." That being said, she needed to step up her job search just in case. And she probably needed a nap before she went off on anyone else.

"Okay, then. The guys were talking earlier before you got here, and we made plans to go to Bachelor this afternoon. You up for it? Since we've finished eating, we thought now would be a good time to head up there."

Absolutely not. Bailey pushed her glasses higher on her nose. "What about cleanup?"

"The guys and Sarah are putting the food away right now. Mark and I can do the dishes later. He said he'd come back and help."

"Okay." Bailey twisted the knob and pulled the door open.

She stifled a yawn. After working in the kitchen half the day, all she wanted to do was put her feet up. But inner tubing sounded like fun, and she didn't want to disappoint her friends.

A short while later, they piled into Mark's car and headed up the mountain. The parking lot was nearly full, but they managed to find a spot. The five of them got out of the black sub-compact and trekked through the lot.

Bailey turned to look behind her for cars as they crossed the lane and gasped. Her legs turned to jelly. Was that the same silver car that had been behind her a few days ago? She tried to get a glimpse of the driver, but couldn't even tell if it was a man or a woman.

"You coming, Bailey?" Nicole asked from a few steps ahead of her.

"Ah." She turned to them, then back toward the car, which pulled into a spot. "Right behind you." She double-timed it. No way did she want to be left alone.

"Miss Davis! Bailey!" A familiar young voice called.

Bailey stifled a groan. The conversation with the girl's uncle still fresh in her mind, she turned and looked for the voice's owner, Lacy Belafonte. About ten cars away Lacy jumped up and down, waving.

Bailey's heart warmed to the sweet girl who rarely let her excitement show.

Nicole whispered in her ear. "You don't have to deal with that family anymore today if you smile, wave, and keep walking."

"Easy for you to say, you're only Lacy's teacher. I live with her grandmother. Besides, she's a sweet girl. It will only take a minute to say hi. You and Sarah can go ahead. I'll catch up."

"What about Stephen?" she whispered too loudly.

Mark chuckled and placed a kiss on Nicole's forehead. "Stay and lend moral support. Besides, there's safety in numbers.

Spencer and I will buy tickets for the inner tube tow."

Bailey pressed her lips together. Mark was a cop and was always touting safety in numbers—as if it even applied in this situation. Lacy wasn't a threat. Bailey gulped when she spotted Stephen and the frown that tugged at his mouth. On second thought she could use moral support. Time to get this over with. She pulled Nicole and Sarah along with her toward Lacy, Stephen, and John. The two brothers looked nothing alike. Stephen had thick, dark hair with deep blue eyes, and a medium build, where John's hair was wavy. His eyes were light blue, and he was built like a linebacker.

Stephen rested a hand on his niece's shoulder, and the group walked toward them.

Bailey spoke out of the side of her mouth, never taking her gaze off Stephen. "Coming here was a bad idea."

"Oh, stop. You know how I love spinning and whirling down the slope. It's more fun than . . . anything. Besides, it's too late to run away now." Nicole nudged her shoulder. "Next time follow my advice and simply wave."

Bailey stuck her tongue out at her friend.

Lacy and her brother Collin snickered.

"Hi, kids." Nicole greeted them as if they were at school. "Did you have a nice meal?"

"The best." Stephen's gentle voice caressed Bailey's wounded heart. Her gaze flew to his and locked. His look of remorse astonished and confused her. "I'm surprised to see you here."

"Nicole has a thing for inner tubes flying out of control at breakneck speed."

Her friend gently nudged her toward the lodge. "Yep. I'm a daredevil, all right. See you Monday, Lacy." She looped an arm through Sarah's, pivoted, and started walking. "You coming,

Bailey?" She raised a brow.

Bailey glanced toward Nicole then back at the family she'd grown to love—well, grown to love almost all of them. Stephen and his mother were another matter. "Have fun, kids." She waved to the men and carefully jogged after Nicole. "You didn't have to rush off."

"I didn't rush off, exactly. I said hi. I thought if I walked away it'd give you the excuse you needed to escape. Besides, the guys are waiting, and I want to get in line." She shot her a wide grin. "You have no idea how much I love this."

"Hmm. Actually, I think I might." Nicole pulled her toward the lodge at a fast clip until they met the men, who were standing in line. Nicole snuggled against Mark, leaving Bailey and Sarah with Spencer.

"How'd you get talked into this, Spence?" Bailey asked.

He shot her an annoyed glance. "Do you realize you're the only person who gets away with calling me that?"

Sarah chuckled.

Bailey shook her head. "I had no idea. You don't like being called Spence?" She faced the stocky man who she'd met only last month. "Would you rather I call you Spencer?"

He grinned. "Nope. But I get to come up with a nickname for you. I'm thinking Bay."

She wrinkled her nose.

"What? You don't like that?"

"I'm not a body of water, and I prefer my actual name."

"Sorry, fair is fair. How about Bails?"

"No way. If you must use a nickname, Bay is fine. . . Spence." She rolled her eyes and crossed her arms. "But don't expect me to reply."

Spencer chuckled as he connected a blue inner tube to the towrope and eased onto it. Sarah claimed a red one.

Bailey plopped onto a yellow inner tube and rode it to the top. Bailey's friend claimed to love inner tubing, but she knew the truth of the matter was Nicole didn't want to exclude her by skiing. Bailey was terrified of skiing. They had probably planned to ski until she'd shown up. She shivered. The idea of careening down the side of a mountain on two skinny stick-like things, along with hundreds of other people, sent chills of terror through her.

She disconnected from the tow and stood in the line for the closest run. Nicole turned and mouthed, "He's cute" as she pointed to Stephen who walked nearby.

Bailey's eyes widened, and she mouthed back, "Stop." What had gotten into her normally reserved friend? Bailey settled onto her inner tube as Nicole screamed down the run. Bailey pushed off. Wind stung her face, and her eyes watered. She hit a bump and caught air, landed with a quick thud, and kept going to the bottom. Laughing, she rolled off and dragged the tube back to the line.

Stephen stood in front of her. He turned, presumably looking for his family. "Hello again."

"Hi, yourself." Her stomach knotted. Would he cause a scene now that the kids weren't with him? The man was as unpredictable as the inner tube run.

"I saw you with a guy earlier. Is he your boyfriend?"

"He's a friend of a friend." She couldn't decipher the look on his face. Surprise? No, a frown . . . or did he grin? Was he pleased she didn't have a boyfriend? What a confusing man. Good thing his opinion didn't matter.

She pressed her lips together. Who was she kidding? She cared way more than she should. His opinion mattered to her—and that wasn't good. She couldn't help noticing his good looks and how much he cared for his family. But there was something about Stephen that made him mysterious too.

Lacy ran up to them. "This is so much fun. You and Uncle Stephen should go down together. He's the best." She looked at her uncle with adoring eyes.

It appeared Stephen had made a good impression on his niece.

"Let's go, squirt," John tugged on Lacy's braid. "We can race down to the bottom."

Stephen's deep bass voice grabbed her attention again. "My brother is as big a kid as my niece and nephew. He'll be out here with them until they close the run. You want to get a cup of coffee or hot chocolate later? My treat."

"Why?" She'd expected him to at least wait until Monday to fire her.

"I want to apologize for my phone call earlier."

"Oh?" She studied his face more closely.

Regret filled his eyes. "Yes. I should never have called you. I was frustrated with my family and took it out on you. I'm very sorry and wish to make it up to you, at least in a small way."

"What'd you have in mind?"

"Coffee?"

Indecision gripped her. She wanted to say yes, but it wasn't wise to spend any more time with him than necessary. He was, after all, a Belafonte. Then again if the situation were reversed, she'd want him to say yes. "Okay. Let's meet at the lodge in an hour."

"Thanks!" A smile lit his face. "I'll see you later."

A tingle of excitement rose. She had a coffee date. *Ack.* It wasn't a date—just coffee, even if she wished it were more there was no way he'd ever think of her like that.

CHAPTER FIVE

Stephen stood at the top of the inner tube run. Childlike giddiness raced through him, but he was ready for a break. He checked the time—last run. He pushed off and zoomed down the run. Snowflakes blinded him and hit his face like a million tiny pinpricks. He finally came to a stop at the bottom where his niece and nephew waited. "I'm going to meet someone for coffee. The two of you need to stay with Uncle John."

"Who are you meeting?" Lacy asked.

He tapped her nose. "Bailey, if you must know."

Her eyes gleamed approval. "She's really nice."

"So you've said. Call or text if you need me."

She nodded then dragged her brother off toward John. She turned and waved. A big smile lit her face.

Stephen spotted Bailey outside the store near the inner tube park talking with her friends. Good. He had hoped to find her, since he'd made a change in plans. He tromped across compacted snow then sidled up behind her and waited for her to stop talking. Her alto voice held a warmth he hadn't noticed before.

"Nicole, I'm heading to the lodge to warm up with coffee. I'll catch up with everyone later." Bailey yanked off her gloves and stuffed them into her jacket pocket.

Nicole flicked a glance his way with a raised brow. "Okay. Where's Spencer?"

"He spotted friends and took off with them. He said to call when we're ready to leave."

"Will do." Nicole rested a hand on Bailey's arm and lowered her voice so Stephen could barely hear her words. "You okay?"

"Of course. Have fun!" She whirled around and ran smack into him then stumbled backward. Stephen grasped Bailey's shoulders to steady her.

"Sor—Stephen." She stepped back. "I thought we were meeting in the lodge." Her eyes lit, bringing out flecks of gold in the hazel. She looked puzzled.

"I thought of a better idea I hope you'll like." He shivered and rubbed his hands together. "I'm more than ready to warm up."

"Me too." A snowflake landed on the tip of her nose and didn't melt.

She must be freezing.

"My gloves are completely soaked, and my hands are like ice." She plowed through the snow beside him. "Do you mind if I ask you a question?"

He raised an eyebrow. "Go ahead."

"What's wrong with me going a little above and beyond for your family? They've been through a lot in the past couple of months. I could have said no if I'd wanted to."

He tilted his head. "Really? I'm not so sure. Saying no to my family seems to be difficult for you." He sighed. He'd wanted to apologize, not cause more strife between them.

"You don't know me, Stephen. Perhaps I *was* looking forward to the meal, but I also enjoyed spending time with my friends, so it all worked out. And for the record, I like my job—at least I do most of the time. Am I asked to do some odd things for Mona? On occasion. But I'm her assistant. As such, I pick up the slack. Lots of assistants do odd jobs for their bosses. This isn't as big of a deal as you seem to think."

"Not during the holidays. Cooking a holiday meal goes well

beyond picking up the slack. And I doubt most bosses would even ask. But I get your reason for doing it. Thank you for caring so much."

"You're welcome." Relief covered her face. "But I think next year I'll leave the cooking to you so you can show off some of those French cooking skills you learned." She shot him a cheeky grin.

"Touché. As for taking care of my brother's kids, don't let them take advantage of your kindness. You work for my mom, not Judy."

"Technically true, but your mom was their childcare until she had her stroke, so I inherited them."

Ah. Now he understood. Then why was his mom so negative toward Bailey? It made zero sense. He needed to get his mother to see reason and the big picture—their company needed Bailey whether Mom would admit it or not. Her health was not improving, and Bailey was the glue that held the designing part of the family business together. "I took the liberty of purchasing us each a lift ticket up to Pine Marten Lodge. The view from The Cirque restaurant is pretty amazing. Plus, I hear they have great pies."

Bailey grinned. "That sounds wonderful. We skipped dessert today, and I've worked up an appetite. Didn't you enjoy the pies I bought?"

He patted his stomach. "I did, but I'm a bit of a dessert hog." He almost laughed at how wide her eyes grew. Clearly he'd taken her by surprise.

They stood in line and were soon whisked up onto the chairlift. The snow stopped, but a brisk wind shot cold that reached his bones. Skiers swooshed down the mountainside below them. "It's colder than I expected."

"Me too," Bailey said.

A few minutes later they stepped off the chairlift. He'd read the restaurant was the highest in Oregon at 7,800 feet. On a clear day, the view must be amazing.

Bailey's teeth chattered, and her body shook as they walked toward the building.

"Are you okay?" The long ride up had been breezy and especially cold—so much for warming up. Maybe his great plan wasn't so wonderful after all. The lodge down below would have been fine. He hadn't intended to turn her to ice.

She nodded and picked up the pace toward the lodge. Good thing it was close to the lift. He lengthened his stride to match her steps to the entrance. Hot air smacked him in the face as he followed Bailey inside.

"It feels so good in here. I might even start to feel my toes again, if we stay very long," she said through chattering teeth.

He chuckled. "Good point. We should order pie and tell them to keep the coffee coming."

"Sounds perfect." They sat at a table beside a window. Bailey caught her breath. "Look, it's starting to snow again. I can't believe this view." Her rosy cheeks matched the excitement in her voice. "It's so beautiful up here."

"Mmm." His gazed rested on her. "You don't come up here often?"

She shook her head. "Never. I don't ski. Besides, your mother keeps me very busy, especially now."

"About that. I'm worried about her. She's not herself." He knew the chances of her health returning to its pre-stroke condition weren't likely, but he still held out hope she'd one day be the person he remembered before fleeing to France. "Her demeanor is completely changed. What happened?"

Bailey pressed her lips tightly together as if debating her next words. Her gaze met his. "I think she's angry and embarrassed. It must be frustrating to be dependent on others for simple tasks. I'm not an expert in psychology, but I know I'd be angry to be stuck in that situation, and way past embarrassed."

His mother's insistence that he find a replacement for Bailey seemed to support her observation. Could it be Mom was embarrassed that her assistant had to help her with personal needs? "Now that you mention it, you could be right. My mom is a prideful woman, and I'm sure asking you for help was humiliating." While they ate their apple pie in silence, he couldn't help but wonder why Bailey continued to be so kind to his mom considering everything. He wanted to ask why she didn't quit and go work for their competition, but he didn't want to put any ideas in her head if she hadn't thought of it already.

Bailey was a huge asset to his family and their business, and he didn't want her to leave. He'd viewed some of her work via the gallery Mona kept online and was quite impressed with Bailey's vision. Now if he could only get his mother to realize what they had in her. How could he convince his mom that Bailey was an asset and not a liability?

Bailey stood in the middle of the cold basement the day after Thanksgiving. Sore didn't begin to describe how she felt. Who would have thought inner tubing and playing in the snow could make her so uncomfortable? She definitely needed to join a gym. She was too young to feel like this.

She looked around the dusty space and blew her breath out in a puff. Why her boss stored Christmas decorations in this damp space she would never understand. She bent and groaned as she hoisted a plastic storage box into her arms then trekked upstairs to the main level. One thing was certain, she would work off yesterday's feast with all the trips she would be taking up and down the stairs today.

Too bad no one was around to help. Stephen had taken Mona to physical therapy, so she'd have the place to herself for the next couple of hours.

She stood amongst a dozen boxes. How could she do this alone? It had taken Mona and her days to deck out this place for Christmas last year. She needed her own assistant, but no way would she ask for one. Mona was in an even worse mood than usual when she'd left the house for her appointment, and she was never pleasant after physical therapy.

At least Bailey knew exactly how her boss liked her house decorated. She connected her iPod to the speaker on the main level then cranked up the volume to her favorite Christmas album and sang along with *Angels We Have Heard on High*. From the top of a twelve-foot ladder, she hung mistletoe above the entryway and topped it off with a delicate red bow.

As she climbed down the ladder, she spotted a man walking to the door. She looked more closely and frowned. *Why is Spencer here?* She pulled open the door. "Long time no see. Is everything okay?"

"Yes." He brought his hands out from behind his back.

She sucked in a breath. "Who are the flowers for?" He held a bouquet of red roses.

"You. And they're not from me." He quickly added after thrusting them toward her.

"If they aren't from you, then who?" She suddenly realized how cold it was outside. "Come in for a minute and warm up."

"Okay. Sure." He followed her inside and closed the door behind him. He blew out a slow whistle. "This place is something else. Are you the decorator?"

"I did the Christmas stuff." She pulled the card from the bouquet and placed the flowers on a nearby table. "Roses for a sweet lady." She turned the card over. "It doesn't say who they're from."

"Looks like you have a secret admirer, Bails."

"I thought we agreed to Bay or Bailey. Not Bails."

"Just kidding. Well, my work here is done. I'll be seeing you."

"Wait! You must know who they're from."

He shook his head. "Beats me. They were sitting on Mark's desk. I had to head out this way for something else and offered to drop them by. And before you get weird, I asked, and they are not from Mark."

"Good. I'd hate to tell Nicole she was engaged to a scoundrel. But why would they be at the police station, and why would they be on Mark's desk?"

"It's a mystery to me." Spencer turned toward the door. "Catch you later."

"Okay. Thanks. 'Bye." She found a vase for the flowers and put them in water. The flowers, though a kind gesture, kind of creeped her out. Why would someone leave flowers at the police station for her? Then again, if the person had access to Mark's desk, he couldn't be too bad. At least that's what she wanted to believe. Spencer sincerely seemed to be clueless about who they were from, but how could that be?

On her way to get the ladder she noticed the mistletoe had fallen. It looked as if she needed to try again. She climbed the ladder and retied the ribbon around the hook in the ceiling. The flowers situation troubled her, even though it should have made her happy. After the incident with the silver car she'd been on edge, which was irrational, but she couldn't help herself.

She leaned back to make sure the mistletoe looked perfect.

The ladder wobbled. She grasped the edges with both hands, and then her world teetered. She squealed and squeezed her eyes shut. The ladder jerked to a stop and righted.

"Easy there." Stephen braced the ladder with both hands. "How about you come down from there before you break your neck?" He stayed planted at the bottom.

"Stephen." Her heart thumped wildly. "Thank you! I didn't hear you come in. Where's Mona? Wait, how'd you get in? There's no way you came in that door without me noticing."

He shook his head. "I saw you through the window, so I used the door in the kitchen. My mom is at the hospital. The physical therapist had a concern, so she insisted my mom see her doctor. It turns out Mom has a blood clot in her leg, as well as an infection." Worry filled his eyes.

"Oh, no!" Bailey climbed down one rung at a time, doing her best to ignore her sore muscles. Her foot missed the next. She gasped.

"Easy now. Raise your foot an inch and you'll be there."

She felt for the rung, found it and climbed the rest of the way down.

Stephen released the ladder and took a step away once her feet were nearly on solid ground.

She turned to face him, resting a hand on his arm. "Is there anything I can do?"

He shook his head. "I stopped by to pick up a few things she asked for. Mom's doctor admitted her." He took another step back, causing her hand to drop off his arm, then stopped. "My mother always spoke highly of you and your work before her accident. I hope you will stay on, but it's only fair you should know that she's asked me to replace you."

Bailey gasped. "Are you firing me?"

Pain crossed his face. "No. I . . . I'm sorry. This isn't coming out right. That's not what I was trying to say at all. I meant the opposite, in fact. I've looked at your online portfolio, and it's exceptional. You are a talented designer whose time is more than likely being wasted as my mom's girl Friday."

"Oh." So he liked her work, but why did . . . She shook her head. "I'm very confused. Why does Mona want to get rid of me?"

"I believe you were right about the reason her attitude has turned hostile toward you. My mom is a prideful woman and asking you to help her with personal matters has been humiliating for her. Seeing you reminds her of that and rubs salt into her humble pie, and it doesn't taste good."

So she'd been right. Mona was acting out because she was embarrassed.

"However, regardless of what Mom wants, *we* need you. Our clients know you, and you know our business. I'd like for you to put feelers out for an assistant for yourself. My mom won't be able to work in the foreseeable future, and we need to keep things running as smoothly as possible. You're in charge of the design aspect of the business now, and you'll need someone to take care of running errands and whatever else you did for my mom. Once she is able to come home, I'll hire a nurse or a companion with medical training to live here, so you'll be relieved of her care. That ought to ease the tension between the two of you."

Bailey opened her mouth, but no sound came out. He wouldn't ask her to find an assistant if he thought his mother was going to recover. "How serious is this infection and clot?"

"It's not good. She could die if the clot goes to her heart." His voice caught, and he cleared his throat. "The doctor thinks we caught the infection in time. If we did, then depending on the blood clot situation, she may be home in time for Christmas, but he warned that I needed to make other arrangements for the business. Apparently, the stress is too much for her health."

"I'm so sorry, Stephen. If there is anything at all I can do other than finding an assistant, please let me know. Your family is like a second family to me, and I want to help. What will your mom say when she finds out you didn't fire me?"

His gaze cleared, and it looked as though he saw her with new eyes. "I'll tell her how it is. I'm hoping she will come to her senses. Thank you, for not getting angry and for offering to help." He rushed past her and up the stairs. He stopped at the top and turned. "I've thought of something you could do."

"Anything." Anyone willing to stand up to Mona on her behalf had her loyalty.

"Make this the best Christmas ever. And let me know what you need. Oh, and if you don't mind continuing to stay at the house, it would make me feel better knowing this place isn't empty."

"Okay." She blinked back tears. Based on Stephen's request, it sounded as if this would in all likelihood be Mona's last Christmas. She squared her shoulders, determined to fulfill Stephen's request. This would be a Christmas to remember.

"I saw roses in the kitchen."

Her stomach knotted. "Yes. Apparently I have a secret admirer."

He raised a brow. "Any idea who?"

"No. Hence the word secret." She forced a smile. The last thing Stephen needed was to know how weirded-out those flowers made her.

He nodded. "Well, I need to get moving."

"Okay." She kicked up the pace and soon the kinks had worked out of her body. Tuning out all her worries, she threw her concentration into decorating. She glanced toward the window and realized it was dark. What time was it? She pulled out her cell phone. "Seven!" Where had the time gone? She'd finished the entryway, staircase, and great room, but it'd taken all day. Ready to drop, she kicked off her shoes and sank into the couch. They still needed a Christmas tree. Maybe Stephen could have one delivered. She had a consultation at nine in the morning and then needed to visit one of the job sites along with a plethora of other tasks.

The doorbell pealed. In the time she had been living here, no one had ever rung the bell. Her mind shot to the flowers—no, her admirer wouldn't come ringing her employer's doorbell–unless he'd hoped to catch her alone. It was probably common knowledge by now that Mona had been hospitalized. Enough of this paranoia. She stood and rushed to the door, trying to ignore her protesting muscles.

Stephen stood there with slightly slumped shoulders.

Relief washed over her.

"I wanted to let you know I'm back and see if everything went okay. No more ladder mishaps?"

She grinned in spite of feeling ready to drop. "Not a one." She opened the door wider. "I can't believe it, but I'm about finished with the decorations. Which reminds me. We need a tree. There is a grower-direct lot in Bend, so the trees last a long time. Do you think you could have one delivered sometime this week? I'll be out all day tomorrow, but if you're free . . ." She pressed her lips together. "Sorry. I ramble when I'm tired."

A soft grin lifted his lips. "I'll make sure there's a tree, but I'm not paying someone to deliver one that I didn't pick out myself. Let's plan to visit a tree lot this weekend." He walked into the house. "Do you mind if I see what you did?"

"Of course not." She moved aside.

He stood in the center of the entryway directly below the mistletoe where he had a perfect view of the main floor. She hadn't tackled upstairs and had no plans to either. "It's perfect.

Mom will love it."

"She'd better. I took pictures during the past two Christmases for reference. She does it the same way every year. This is your mother's design."

He really looked at her for the first time since coming to the door, and a twinkle lit his eyes. "You sure get into your work."

Her stomach lurched. She glanced in the hall mirror, and her eyes widened. Dust streaked across her nose, and glitter decorated her hair. "I'm a mess." She was ugly enough, without adding to it. She sighed. Why hadn't he laughed at her? She'd known a few people who would have. Then again, he wasn't a cruel person.

"Come here."

She moved toward him, uncertainty causing her to move extra slow.

He chuckled. "I don't bite. You look terrified." He pulled what looked to be a clean hanky from his pocket and wiped the top of her nose. "Much better," he said softly as he stuffed the cloth back in his pocket. "Bailey?"

"M-hmm."

"Breathe."

She let out the breath she'd been holding and prayed he wouldn't look up and notice they stood below the mistletoe.

He moved toward the door and turned back. "The mistletoe is a nice touch. See you later, Miss Sparkles." He winked and sauntered outside.

She snapped her jaw closed. What was it with men and nicknames? In spite of her annoyance, she couldn't stop the grin that spread across her face. Maybe the glitter *helped* her appearance. She couldn't wait until Saturday!

CHAPTER SIX

STEPHEN KICKED SNOW OFF HIS BOOTS and stepped into his cabin, still grinning from his encounter with Bailey. She sure knew how to wear her work. She'd probably be washing glitter out of her hair for days. Considering the hours she worked, he was surprised she'd managed to catch the eye of an admirer. Then again, any man who cared to notice would see she was a remarkable woman.

He took off his winter gear and stowed it in the closet then moved to the kitchen. He sobered as he opened the fridge and spotted turkey leftovers. Had Thanksgiving only been yesterday? Mom had seemed fine, except for eating next to nothing. Apparently she had been hiding a couple of things. He grabbed a bottle of water and closed the door.

Suddenly tired, he moved into the living room and collapsed on the couch. The day had gone nothing like he'd planned. Coming home wasn't supposed to be this hard.

He looked over at the mantle, and Rebecca's picture grabbed his attention. "You would never believe what's going on. Mom is a mess . . . I'm a mess." He ran a hand over his face and sighed. "I miss you." Rebecca would know what to do. She always knew how to deal with his mother.

His wife wasn't here anymore, and he needed to stop wishing for the way things used to be. He thought he was past the mourning stage, but now the daily reminders from the past were becoming too much. *Lord, how do I move on when every time I turn around something reminds me of Rebecca?*

He stood and tucked her photo behind a vase. Maybe if her gorgeous face wasn't staring at him every time he walked in the door, he would stop wallowing in the past.

He snatched up his cell and punched in Rick's number. "Hey, it's me."

"How's Mom doing?"

"Not great. Has she always been this difficult?"

"Apparently being away for two-and-a-half years has affected your memory. Mom is the orneriest woman I know, but she's probably scared and that's causing her to be more difficult— at least that's Judy's take."

"More than likely your wife is right. I'd be scared if I were in Mom's situation."

"I think most people would be. How are things going with Bailey? I still can't believe Mom told you to let her go. Did something happen with a client?"

"No. Nothing like that. Honestly, I think it has more to do with Mom's pride than anything. Bailey is an exceptional designer. Mom is in no state of mind to be hiring or firing. Although she did say something about a client preferring not to have Bailey on the site."

"What?"

"It's nothing. The woman is a snob. Apparently she expects her designer to look a certain way, and Bailey doesn't fit her expectations." He'd admit that the woman didn't go all out with her appearance, but when a person got into their work the way she did, it was probably for the best. Her dry cleaning bill would be astronomical.

"Hmm, well that's too bad. Personally, I like Bailey's work. She's easy to deal with. And once she makes up her mind about a detail, she rarely changes it, which is great from my point of view."

"So you're comfortable with Bailey filling Mom's shoes. At least for now? I took the liberty of telling Bailey to hire an assistant. If she's going to take over the design side of the business, she'll need help." Silence met his ears. Had he made a mistake usurping his mother's authority? His shoulders tightened. "Rick? Are you still there?"

"Yeah, it just hit me that we could lose Mom, and I'm not ready for that to happen."

"Me neither."

"I like Bailey and all, but shouldn't one of us choose her assistant?"

Stephen frowned. "I see your point, but I think it's important for Bailey to find someone she's comfortable working with. That being said, I'll sit in on those interviews."

"Good idea, even though Bailey is a great designer and her ideas are fresh, I'd like one of us to have a say in who we bring into the business."

He made a mental note to talk to Bailey about setting up interviews. "Did you fill John in on what happened?"

"Yes, and don't worry. Mom's strong and a fighter. If anyone can make a comeback, it's her."

"Agreed. Thanks for stepping in and helping with everything else. I've been swamped with work and things with Judy have been rocky."

Stephen's stomach knotted. This was the first he'd heard of his brother's marital problems. "Not that I'm a marriage expert, but if you need someone to talk to . . ."

"Thanks, but this is something Judy and I need to work out privately."

"I understand." Stephen made plans to meet with his brothers the next day and placed his phone on the counter. Rick was a good older brother and excellent at managing the construction side of the family business. Stephen appreciated the open acceptance Rick had offered when he came home and how his brother had told him he could step back into his role heading up the architect and design side of the business whenever he was ready. Not all families would have been so gracious to the prodigal son who took off to heal when his world fell apart.

He was happy to be home. Even though the daily reminders of Rebecca were painful at times, he needed to be with his family, and Mom's assistant fit right in with them.

An image of Bailey's dirt-streaked face danced in his mind—adorable. He chuckled, then sobered, shaking off the thought. Not that he wasn't open to the idea of someday falling in love again but now wasn't the time. Things were too uncertain with his mother, and he needed to reestablish himself in the family business and the community.

Late Friday afternoon, Bailey sat at the desk in her bedroom at Mona's house, facing the only window. She pressed enter on the keyboard and grinned. The online ad for an assistant was officially posted. Hopefully she'd start receiving résumés soon. Without Mona, everything would fall on her, and running Belafonte Designs was too big for one person. She worried her bottom lip. What if she hired the wrong person? She knew nothing about conducting an interview. She reached for her cell phone and called home. "Hi, Mom."

"It's about time I heard from you. I tried reaching you yesterday afternoon to see how the meal went, but your phone went straight to voicemail. Did you have a nice day with the

Belafontes?"

Bailey sighed. "Not really. I guess I misunderstood Mona's invitation. She asked me to leave once I was finished cooking."

"Of all the insensitive, unkind —"

"Mom, calm down. My friend Nicole invited me to her place. Her fiancé and his buddy were there, along with another friend. After we ate, we all went to Mt. Bachelor to inner tube. I had a lot of fun." She liked Nicole's friend Sarah, and the three of them had plans to go Christmas shopping this weekend.

"Oh, well, I'm glad you have good friends, but what your boss did was rotten."

"True, but Mona hasn't been herself since her stroke. She's back in the hospital."

"I'm sorry to hear that, and I'm sorry I lost my temper."

"It's okay. Did you happen to send me red roses?" She stared out her bedroom window that faced Stephen's cabin, the roofline visible through a break in the trees. Between the roses and the silver car she was becoming a little paranoid. She kept telling herself she was imagining things, and that she needed to stop reading thrillers. Silver was a popular color for a car, but that sure had looked like the same car.

"I didn't send any. Someone sent you flowers?" Her voice hitched in excitement.

"Yes, but they didn't sign the card."

"What did it say?"

"Roses for a sweet lady. If that's not odd enough, they were delivered by Spencer." She'd mentioned the man to her mother before, so there was no need to go into it now.

"Do you think they're from him?"

"No." Spencer wouldn't lie. From what she'd seen of him, he lived in a black and white world. He'd own up to the flowers . . . unless he was trying to be a secret Santa. Hmm. She far preferred the idea of Spencer being a secret Santa to some mystery person in a silver car.

Mom's voice drew her from her thoughts. "Your dad and I can't wait to see you on Christmas."

"I'm looking forward to coming home. It's been too long." She used to get over the Santiam pass to Salem at least once a month, but since Mona's stroke, she'd been needed here. They visited for another twenty minutes before promising to talk again on the following Friday.

Bailey reached for a Christmas book she'd purchased in October and moved over to the steel-gray armchair beside her desk. Good thing it was a sweet romance rather than another thriller. She turned it around to face the window and snuggled into the seat. A gentle snow, not more than a mist, cascaded from the sky, sparkling in the moonlight. The beauty of Central Oregon caused her creativity to work overtime. She set the unopened book aside, slipped off her glasses, and closed her eyes, envisioning the exact shape and size of the Christmas tree she wanted for the house.

Mona might not be the kindest woman, but she hadn't always been like that. Bailey determined this would be a Christmas to remember for her boss. This house would be decorated to the nines. Her muscles relaxed into the cushiony seat.

Bailey's eyes flew open—darkness shrouded her room. She must have fallen asleep. Her heart pounded. What had awaked her? She listened, straining to understand why her heart was pounding.

Were those footsteps on the wood floor downstairs? She looked around the bedroom for a weapon, and the only thing that looked even somewhat lethal was a silver candlestick. Grabbing it from the dresser, she slunk to the door and peered out. She tiptoed down the hall toward the staircase.

Glass shattered. A deep voice said something unintelligible.

A small scream escaped, and she slapped a hand over her mouth. She should have called the police and hidden. Maybe it wasn't too late. The lights were off all around her, but moonlight illuminated the interior via the skylights, allowing her to see easily enough. Wait—that couldn't all be from the moon—a light shone in the great room. A burglar wouldn't turn a lamp on—at least a smart one wouldn't.

Every part of her wanted to dash back to her room, call the police, and hide under the covers, but whoever was here needed to be dealt with now. The outline of a person came into view as he moved toward the door. Suddenly he dropped, and a thud sounded. He groaned. Her pulse thrummed in her ears. With a shaking hand, she reached for the stairway light switch and flipped it up. "Stephen! What are you doing?" Her voice sounded strained.

He lay sprawled on the floor near the front door. A box of Christmas decorations tipped on its side and several ornaments still rocked back and forth on the hardwood floor. It looked like a few glass bulbs had shattered, but it was difficult to be certain since she'd forgotten to slip on her glasses and details were fuzzy. His face reddened, and he sat up. "I . . . that is . . . hmm. This is really embarrassing."

She trotted down the stairs. "Are you hurt?"

"Only my pride." He staggered to his feet. "Watch out for the glass."

She missed the last stair and stumbled into his arms. She caught her breath, and she willed her pulse to slow. His warm arms gently released her, making her wish he still held her. She stepped back. "Sorry. I'm not wearing my glasses and missed that last step." Why was she always falling into this man? She must be more careful!

"Glad I was here to catch you." He winked, then sobered. "Sorry for waking you. I couldn't sleep and thought I'd surprise you, only not like this. It appears I slipped on the tree needles that fell off as I brought the tree inside."

"Tree?"

"What do you think?" He motioned toward the great room to their left. A huge Douglas fir stood where Mona always displayed a tree.

"It's nice, but I thought we were going to the lot together tomorrow." Disappointment thickened her throat. She'd really looked forward to picking out the tree.

"I know, but you work so hard, and I have all this energy built up. I wanted to do something to make your life a little easier. Especially after yesterday."

She waved the hand holding the candlestick. "Forget about yesterday. You apologized, and I accepted. End of story." She frowned toward the tree. Maybe she shouldn't judge it without her glasses, but from what she could see, Mona wouldn't approve. "I appreciate your effort, but that scraggly tree doesn't work for this room."

"Scraggly! I beg to differ. This tree is perfect. You need to look at it with your glasses on."

"Perhaps, but I'm the designer, remember. Mona always buys a Noble Fir from a lot. I can easily tell that's not a Noble."

He crossed his arms. A scowl covered his face.

"I've had a long day, my back hurts, and I'm beat. Do what you want, but make sure your mom knows you did it and not me." She whirled around and marched up the stairs. "Please lock up on your way out." She called over her shoulder then turned. "And you can't come in here at all times of the day or night. Not if your mom isn't here. You're going to give me a heart attack."

A soft chuckle turned into an all-out laugh. "Lady, you are

not at all what I thought you were. I'll take the tree with me to my place. Mom probably *would* prefer a Noble Fir."

She turned slowly, then slunk back down the stairs. "It's late. This will keep until morning, including the broken bulb." The mantle clock read ten minutes to midnight.

"Remember—can't sleep." He pointed to his gorgeous deep blue eyes.

"Right." She pressed her lips together then squared her shoulders. "I'll help."

"Oh no, you won't. I managed to get the tree in here on my own, I can get it out."

"Then I'll carry the ornaments."

"Nice try. I'll get those too."

She shook her head. "It will take you forever, and I won't be able to sleep until this place is locked up. You may not have anything pressing first thing in the morning, but I have a consultation, and I need my sleep. I'll put the box on the front porch, so you won't need to come back inside." She held out her hand.

"What?"

"The key." Palm out, she wiggled her fingers.

"You're being ridiculous, but if it helps you to sleep, I promise to not use my key except in case of an emergency." He raised a brow challenging her to argue.

Maybe she was overreacting, but it really did freak her out to have someone in the house at all hours of the night. How was she to know he wasn't a burglar? But based on the firm look on his face, he wouldn't relinquish his key. She lowered her hand. "Fine. I'll get the broom and dustpan." She whirled around and marched to the utility closet. She glanced in a large mirror resting against a wall on the way and cringed. Her wild hair and mascara-induced raccoon eyes gave her the look of a maniac. Though tempted to sneak into the guest bathroom and make herself more presentable, she instead grabbed the broom and dustpan.

"You get lost?" Stephen came up behind her.

She squealed. "Will you please stop scaring me?"

He chuckled. "I'm really sorry. I'm not meaning to." He rubbed the back of his neck, tilting his head to the side and giving her a sheepish smile.

Bailey grinned. "Apology accepted." She thrust the cleaning supplies into his hand. "But you get the honors."

"No problem." He brushed the shards into a pile.

Five minutes later, the glass was cleaned up. She helped him carry the tree outside as far as the porch.

"I'll get it from here. Thanks." He turned and dragged the tree through the snow toward his cabin.

She placed the box outside and slid the lock into place. A small smile tipped her lips as she headed to bed. She'd been a little hard on Stephen, but he didn't seem to mind. Life around the Belafonte house had turned interesting since his arrival. What would the man do next?

CHAPTER SEVEN

SATURDAY AFTERNOON, STEPHEN FOLLOWED BAILEY DOWN a row of Christmas trees. Carolers serenaded shoppers near an outdoor fireplace as young children scampered between the rows of trees. He could imagine his niece and nephew doing the same. "How about this one." He pulled a seven-foot Noble Fir from the stand and held it upright.

She circled the tree and shook her head. "Nope. It needs to be fuller on the bottom."

He hadn't realized what an overachiever the woman was. His own tree, though imperfect, fit his cabin perfectly; at least it did once he cut off the bottom two feet.

After he'd dragged it to his home, he was too tired to decorate and left the tree natural. The ornaments Bailey left on the porch were his mom's anyway. He needed to get decorations of his own. Rebecca hadn't been a fan of Christmas and never wanted a tree. She thought they were too messy. "When we're done here, do you mind stopping someplace to purchase ornaments and lights?"

She shook her head. "Of course not, but your mom has plenty."

"I was thinking of picking up some for my tree."

Bailey stopped and faced him. "You don't have any?"

He shook his head.

A thoughtful look crossed her face. "Then why did you leave the box of ornaments on the porch?"

"Those are my mom's decorations. I want my own."

"I didn't think of that." She pushed her glasses up higher on her perfect nose and pressed her lips together. "You know what would be fun?"

"Hmm?" For some reason the image of her from his late night visit filled his mind, and he held back a laugh. Her look today was a far cry from her disheveled appearance last night. Today she wore crisp looking jeans with brown boots that went to her knees, along with a hunter green jacket. Her hair hung loose down her back, somewhat disheveled but still managed to appear soft and shiny. He reached his hand up to touch it, then stopped. What was he doing? He couldn't touch her hair. He dragged his gaze away from her hair and focused on her face.

Excitement shone in Bailey's eyes. "Since your tree is so rustic, it would be neat to use all homemade ornaments and colored lights. You could have the kids come over and make an afternoon of creating ornaments for your tree."

"That sounds like fun, but do you think Lacy and Collin would agree?"

She nodded. "Oh yeah. Those two had a blast helping me decorate last year."

He frowned. It seemed even before his mother's stroke, Bailey spent a great deal of time with his entire family. No wonder the kids loved her. "Does Judy ask you to watch the kids a lot?"

"More now that she's working fulltime, but I offered to watch them last Christmas so she could shop and not have to worry about picking them up from school. We made a party out of it. Your mom loved it." She chuckled, and her face took on a dreamy expression. "Mona had the kids stringing popcorn and berries. They had their own small tree to decorate. Later that night after I went home, they watched Christmas movies until late. Lacy said they ended up spending the night." She shook her head, as if coming back to reality, gave him a disarming smile, and strolled up the next aisle.

He'd missed so much. Regret washed over him, and he determined now, even more than before, to make this year a Christmas to remember.

"Perfect!" She grinned and pointed.

The tree stood at least three feet taller than his nearly six feet. "It's a giant."

"Yes, and your mom will love it."

He pulled out his wallet. "Okay." He made arrangements to have the tree delivered the following morning, then spotted Bailey in the parking lot talking with the same guy he'd seen with her at the mountain. She'd said there wasn't anything between them, but now he wondered. He sidled up to her. "All set?"

She smiled, but worry showed in her eyes. "Sure. Stephen, this is my friend Spencer. He's a police officer in Sunriver."

Spencer reached out his hand. "Good to meet you. Bailey tells me you bought the king of all trees."

"She'd be right." Why did he sense unease in Bailey? What had changed from a few minutes ago? Did this Spencer guy make her uneasy?

Spencer chuckled. "Sounds like a lot of work to me." He waved and sauntered off toward the trees.

"Nice guy."

She shrugged. "I don't know him well. He's more of a friend of a friend. You know how that is. So, where to next?" She looked nervously toward the parking lot.

"Everything okay?"

She nodded then shook her head. "See that silver car?"

He looked the direction she indicated. "What about it?"

"I don't know, but I feel like everywhere I go it's there."

Unease settled on him. "Should I try and catch Spencer and

have him check it out?"

"No! Forget I said anything. I'm sure it's only my overactive imagination. It's probably not even the same vehicle."

He glanced toward the car again and noted the make and model. A newer Toyota Camry. He'd keep an eye out. Bailey's concern was enough for him to be extra vigilant—imagination or not. "Okay then. You ready to go to the craft store?"

"Yes."

He noted that the car followed them from the tree lot, but it could be a coincidence. The Camry stayed a few car lengths back, but he never lost sight of it. The knot in his stomach tightened. Why would someone follow Bailey? From what he'd seen of her, she lived a quiet life.

A few miles down the road he signaled and turned into the craft store's parking lot. The silver car kept going. His shoulders relaxed. *Whew!* Bailey's paranoia had rubbed off on him. He parked and escorted her inside.

With Bailey's expertise, they made quick work of buying supplies to decorate his tree then headed home. "Have you made any progress on finding an assistant?"

A frown drew her brows together.

"No, and I'm worried. What if no one sends me their resume?"

"Then expand the search. Advertise outside the area."

"I hadn't thought of that. Thanks." She cleared her throat. "I have a confession to make." She laced her fingers together in her lap. "I could use help decorating Mona's tree. Any chance you'll be free tomorrow?"

His stomach flopped. "I am. I could get a couple of the guys to come over too." Now why had he said that? He held his breath half hoping she'd turn down the offer. He'd much rather have her to himself—It would make getting to know her easier. And maybe he'd get to the bottom of why she thought she was being followed.

"Oh, no," she said. "Between the two of us we'll get the job done. How's your mom doing? I stopped by the hospital yesterday, and they told me only family was allowed to visit, and the nurse wouldn't give me any information."

"She's about the same. The antibiotics are helping the infection, but the blood clot is still a concern."

"I'd like to send flowers. Would that be okay?"

He glanced her way, finding it difficult to believe how nice she was. His mother treated her like dirt, yet she was nothing but kind. Why? Maybe she actually lived out her faith in the Lord. He shook his head. "She has a roomful. Save your money."

"Oh. When you put it like that, I suppose more flowers would only get in the way." She sat beside him without uttering another word.

Twenty minutes later, he pulled to a stop in front of his mom's house. "I had fun. Who would have thought buying a tree from a lot could be enjoyable?" Although being with her had more to do with his enjoyment than anything.

She shook her head. "I know you prefer to cut a tree yourself, but there's something to be said for the convenience of a tree lot."

"True enough." He reached into the back seat for her bags at the same moment as she did. Their gazes locked. Her cheeks bloomed a sweet pink, and her warm breath tickled his cheek. "You have the most amazing hazel eyes," he whispered. "I've never seen flecks of gold like yours." Her full lips parted and drew him in. He froze. What was he doing? He couldn't kiss Bailey!

She blinked and jerked back as if burned. She took her bags from him. "See you tomorrow." She bolted from the car and fled into the house.

Did I offend her? Maybe he should apologize. But no, he'd not said or done anything wrong. Did she realize he'd almost kissed her? An envelope with Bailey's name on it lay on the passenger side floor and grabbed his attention. She must have dropped it.

Bailey dropped the bags to the floor and rested her head against the closed door. Her heart raced. What had happened out there? It almost seemed as though Stephen had wanted to kiss her, but that wasn't possible. No man ever paid her any attention, at least not like that.

She caught her reflection in the entryway mirror and sighed. The same boring reflection stared back at her. Large rimmed glasses that seemed to swallow her eyes, a nose too-big, a pointy chin, and protruding cheekbones—ugly, since the day she was born, according to her cousin and her cousin's friends.

She'd give anything not to have overheard that conversation all those years ago or lived through the years of teasing and torture that followed. The cruel nickname the kids started to call her at school, and the mean notes about how ugly she was, were old fashioned bullying at its finest. The memory was still clear, even though she'd been in the third grade at the time of the sleepover. She closed her eyes as the scene replayed for the billionth time.

"Bailey is so ugly, her parents should have sent her back." Laughter rang out in her cousin's bedroom as she stood on the other side of the closed door. Horrified, she froze, listening to what they really thought about her. The worst part had been that her favorite cousin had agreed with them and even came up with a quip of her own. "Bailey's face belongs in a zoo. I know. Let's call her ape girl." Bailey shook away the memory and startled as liquid dripped onto her hand, and she realized tears slid down her cheeks. She reached for a tissue and dragged it across her face. A sob caught in her throat. She wanted to be pretty and accepted, but instead she was the ugly duckling—the invisible woman in the room.

She let her breath out in a huff and strode into the kitchen for a glass of water. Being sorry for herself only made her feel horrible, and she did not want to feel that way.

The spotless kitchen lifted her spirits. There was nothing like a clean and organized room to help her breathe a little easier. The black quartz countertops sparkled. She grabbed a glass off the open shelf and flicked on the faucet. Cold water filled the glass. She took a sip and set it on the counter with a frown. This big house needed to be filled with a family. It was too quiet.

Tapping on the glass framed door in the kitchen made her jump. She whipped her head around and spotted Stephen. Her stomach sank. She did *not* want to see him right now, but pretending she hadn't seen him wouldn't work.

She flipped the lock and pulled the door open. Cold air rushed in. "What's wrong? And why didn't you go to the front door?" At least then she could have pretended not to hear him knock.

"I tried, but you didn't answer. I started to leave then noticed the light on in the kitchen so I came here instead." He stepped inside, closing the door behind him. "Are you okay?" He ducked his head as if to get on the same eye level. "I didn't upset you did I?"

"Of course not." Bailey kept her shoulder angled toward him and her eyes averted, certain they were red-rimmed. "I'm fine." She cleared her throat. "Did you need something?"

"You dropped this." He held out an envelope with her name on it.

"Thanks, but I've never seen this before." She flipped it over, slid her finger under the flap and across the top, then pulled out a card. She looked at the card with a teddy bear that said Thinking of You across the top.

"Who's it from?"

"Good question." She opened the card and looked inside. "From someone who admires you." Her eyes met Stephen's. Could he have pretended to have found this to make her think someone else had left it? Or had someone jimmied his locks and placed it in his car while they were out today? The silver car had been at the tree lot. She tossed the card onto the countertop as if it'd burned her.

He rubbed his chin and frowned.

"What's wrong?" She knew why *she* was upset, but he couldn't possibly be thinking the same thing.

"I'm trying to figure out how that got in my car, if you didn't put it there."

Maybe Spencer? She shrugged. "It's hard to say. I suppose it could have happened at the tree lot."

"That's where we ran into your friend of a friend."

She nodded.

"Interesting coincidence. Are you sure you can trust him? It's kind of creepy."

She agreed, but having him say it made her all the more freaked out. "Spencer is a cop. I don't think I need to worry about him." She still didn't believe he'd lie to her. It wasn't who he was.

"Okay, but be careful. Oh, I forgot to tell you the Christmas tree will be delivered at eight tomorrow morning. I know it's Sunday, so if that's a problem let me know, and I'll make sure I'm here. I paid extra to have them come in and set it up."

"Tomorrow morning is fine for the tree delivery. I attend the late service at my church, so it won't be a problem. Thanks for letting me know. Is that all?" In emotional overload, she desperately needed time alone to clear her head. She chanced a look his way and nearly burst into tears at the concern on his face. What was wrong with her? She wasn't a weepy person.

"Before I go, I know you said I didn't upset you, yet I'm the only person you've been with for the past several hours, so regardless of what you say, I feel responsible for the red-rimmed eyes I spotted earlier."

Her cheeks burned. "You didn't do anything. It's me. I let an old wound stir up a memory best left in the past."

Relief shown in his eyes as he nodded. "Being alone when your thoughts are haunting you isn't healthy."

Don't I know it. "I'm fine. Really. But I need to get it out of my head." She moved away from the door and grabbed her glass.

He stepped in further. "I'd rather not spend the evening alone in my cabin. Maybe we could keep each other company. There's a good Christmas movie on tonight. How about we make popcorn and watch it together?"

"I don't know." Did he really not want to be alone, or was he saying this for her benefit?

"It's a great movie. One of my favorites—Elf."

She chuckled. "Well, that changes things. Okay. I need to run to my room for a minute. You could pop the corn, and I'll be right back." She darted up the stairs and into the bathroom. One look in the mirror confirmed her fear. Good thing her glasses kept him from having a clear view of her eyes. She took them off and splashed cool water onto her face then touched up her barely-there makeup to get rid of the shine. Good enough.

After a quick detour to her bedroom for the red and white striped slippers she'd won at a white elephant gift exchange last Christmas, she dashed downstairs, following the aroma of fresh popped corn and found Stephen in the great room, the TV tuned in to the movie.

He held out a bowl for her. "Nice slippers." A teasing grin covered his face.

"Thanks." She snuggled into the far corner of the couch unable to stop the grin that spread across her face. She could get used to evenings like this with Stephen. She liked his marshmallow side. She giggled at the thought of him having a marshmallow side. The man was trim and fit—no fluff anywhere.

"What's so funny?"

"Nothing." She tossed a cushion at him. "Shh. I don't want to miss any."

He popped popcorn into his mouth.

Bailey focused on the television doing her best to ignore the handsome man at the opposite end of the couch. He had a nice laugh, and he had a habit of leaning toward the TV during quieter scenes. She enjoyed watching Stephen almost as much as the movie, which happened to be on her top ten list, right behind *A White Christmas.*

An hour-and-a-half later the credits played across the screen. Bailey frowned. "Did you notice there were no commercials? Not that I enjoy commercials, but that was weird."

"As a matter of fact . . ." He pressed a button, and the Blu-ray player spat out a disk.

"You said it was on tonight!" *The sneak.*

"True, but I never said it was on TV. It's part of my mom's Christmas movie collection."

"Hmm. I see how you are."

He chuckled. "I hope you don't mind my deception."

"No. This movie was exactly what I needed. Thank you." There was nothing like a comedy to get her out of a funk— especially this one. The main character Buddy was an inspiration really. He never lost hope, well maybe for a short time, but he was a shining light in a world of too many Grinches. "I loved the decorations Buddy put up too."

"You don't think they were over the top?"

She shook her head. "Maybe the ones in his dad's bedroom were a bit much, but I really liked his creativity and the white color scheme. Someday I hope to be hired to do a white themed Christmas. I have so many ideas. I'd planned to do it at my condo this year, but . . ."

"But my mom changed your plans. If you'd like to go home, it's okay. I didn't even think when I asked you to stay here. I'm sure you have a life you need to get back to."

"It's okay for now. I like it here. Even if this place is too big for one person. Or even two for that matter." If he only knew what she had waiting for her, he never would have made that offer. An empty condo, frozen dinners, and loud neighbors. Staying in this mansion was a dream she'd never imagined possible. "Besides, it's much easier to run the design business from here. No commute." She grinned.

Relief shone in his eyes. "Good. It's settled. See you in the morning, Bailey." He put the Blu-ray away and slipped out the door.

Bailey tilted her head to the side. "Hmm." There was more to that man than she'd realized, and it might be fun peeling back all the layers.

Could Stephen be her secret admirer? He certainly had opportunity since it was his car, but that didn't explain why Spencer had brought the flowers the first time, or why Spencer showed up at the tree lot today. Maybe Nicole would know.

CHAPTER EIGHT

BAILEY STARTLED AWAKE AND CHECKED HER alarm clock. Eight o'clock. "Yikes." She kicked off the sheets and darted for her closet.

Ding dong!

"I'm coming." She grabbed her cuddly, blue bathrobe and charged down the stairs, missing the bottom step again and landing on all fours. "Oomph." *Smart, Bailey.* Too bad Stephen wasn't here to catch her this time. She scampered to the door and yanked it open. "I'm so sorry. I hope you weren't waiting long." A man wearing a Santa hat and a teen boy each held one end of the Noble Fir she'd chosen at the lot.

"Only a couple of minutes. We were about ready to give up though," the guy wearing the Santa hat said. "Do you have the tree stand set up and in place?"

"Umm . . ." She glanced toward the great room where the tree would go and spotted the stand. "Looks like it." Stephen must have set it up last night when he was getting the movie ready.

"Morning!" Stephen, fresh-faced and all smiles strode onto the porch. He raised a brow at Bailey and grinned. "Rough night?"

Bailey's face heated. "I stayed up late baking and forgot to set my alarm. Since you're here, I'll let you take over." She spun around and darted up the stairs.

It seemed the man was destined to see her at her worst. Last night during her pity party, and now all rumpled—not that it really mattered. A handsome man like Stephen probably thought of her more like a sister than a woman he could have feelings for. She pulled jeans and a red, long sleeve Henley top from her closet then fingered her hair into a ponytail to keep it out of her way. She'd change into church clothes later that would be comfortable enough for Christmas shopping with her friends after church.

After slipping on her glasses, she crept down the stairs. Maybe Stephen wouldn't notice her, and she could make a pot of coffee and clear the cobwebs from her head.

Silence filled the house. Had he gone back to his cabin already? Disappointment hit her—silly. But she had to admit she enjoyed his company. She hadn't expected him to come over this morning, so maybe he'd only stopped by to make sure the tree had been delivered. It stood tall in the great room, and a crackling fire burned in the fireplace.

Soft Christmas music along with the scent of coffee floated toward her from the kitchen. "Hello? Stephen, are you here?" She walked into the large space and stopped. Stephen had coffee brewing, and he stood at the stove with a slab of bacon in hand poised over the pan.

He looked her way. "I hope you like bacon and eggs."

"I love bacon, but you don't need to cook for me."

"I overslept too and didn't have time to eat. It's as easy to cook for two as one. I forgot to mention, I called off the companion search for my mom. At least for now."

"Understandable." But what would she do once Mona came home? His mother would need care that she wouldn't know how to give. She'd have to trust that Stephen and his brothers would plan accordingly.

"I'll have this cooked in no time. There's coffee if you want a cup."

"Thanks, but I'll wait. I think I'll take the boxes into the great room while you finish."

"Oh no, you don't. I want a hand in decorating the tree from beginning to end."

"Suit yourself." She poured herself a mug of coffee, added hazelnut creamer and sat at the bar. "Why do you want to help so much?" Her dad had never enjoyed the task, so she assumed most men didn't.

"I've always loved Christmas, and I used to help my mom and brothers decorate the tree when we were kids. I know it's not the same, but I want to do this for her."

Talk about a nice guy. She didn't know men like him existed—at least she hadn't met one with such a tender heart. She was drawn to Stephen like a butterfly to flowers.

He slid a plate piled with bacon, eggs, and toast her direction. "Eat up."

She breathed in deeply. "This smells so good. I wish I could wake up to this every day." She snapped her mouth shut, suddenly realizing how forward she sounded.

He winked. "Bon appétit."

After eating, they headed for the basement where the boxes were stored and made quick work of carrying several plastic ornament storage boxes into the great room.

"Where do we start?" He looked like a lost boy in the clothing department.

"Lights." She pried the lid off a box.

He groaned. "Not my favorite part."

"Mine either, but it's the most important step in decorating a tree." An hour later, white light lit the tree. She stood back and grinned. "Perfect."

"Not bad if I do say so myself. Now we can do what *I* consider the best part. Ornaments!" Without waiting for instructions, he pulled open the ornament box closest to him with the excitement of a kid ripping into a present.

"Hold on. Your mom has a special way of doing this."

"No she doesn't. We put the ornaments wherever we want." He reached for a Star Wars Jedi ornament.

She shook her head. "Not anymore. She likes only bulbs, and only the oversized ones."

The grin slid off his face. "But what about these? My dad had the whole collection."

She shook her head. "Sorry. Only bulbs."

His crestfallen face tugged at her heart. Would it really hurt to have a few contraband ornaments? "Oh fine. Add them, but keep them on the backside. Maybe she won't notice."

His face lit, then his mouth pulled down in a frown. "Are you sure? I don't want to disappoint my mom."

"I think hanging them on the side she won't see will be fine." At least she hoped Mona wouldn't walk around the tree and give it her usual inspection. "We need Christmas tunes in here." She clicked on the radio and sang along softly to *Silent Night*, a true classic.

"You have a nice voice."

Her gaze darted across the room, where he happily unpacked a mishmash of ornaments. "Thanks." Her mom had always told her she had a nice singing voice, but she'd never believed her. After all, Mom said she was beautiful too, and that wasn't true. Funny, how moms could see what few others did. She shrugged off the thought and pulled out a hand-blown glass bulb Mona had purchased at a gallery last year. It truly was a work of art with waves of varying shades of red.

"That's nice." Stephen now stood only a foot away, a look of awe on his face. "I can see my mother's tastes have elevated since I last helped decorate."

She chuckled. "If those character ornaments are any

indication, I'd say you're right."

"Hey don't knock 'em," he said, playfully. "How about you? What do you hang on your tree?"

She continued to pull large glass bulbs from an ornament bin that kept each one separate and safe and handed one to Stephen. "I don't have a huge collection of ornaments like your mom, so several years ago, I went to the craft store and bought a bunch of different shaped and sized white ones. They are so pretty. Some have glitter, some are frosted, and some are clear. My favorite is a white on white angel bulb."

"Hmm. Your tree is completely white?" He asked the question as if she'd broken some cardinal rule of tree decorating.

"The tree is green. At least it would be if I'd put one up."

The questioning look in his eyes gave her pause.

"Since I'm here this year, there is no need to put up my own tree."

"Ah. So what do you do for fun? It seems you're always working."

"Other than play in the snow, watch movies, shop, and hang out with friends, I don't know. How about you?" She laughed and tossed a wad of crumpled newspaper at him that bounced off his shoulder.

His eyes widened. "Really? I don't think you want to go there. The last time we had a paper fight in this house . . . let's just say things did not end well."

Bailey sobered. "Sorry. My inner-child sometimes gets the best of me." She'd begun to think of him as a friend, but she'd crossed a line.

He grasped the wadded paper and flung it back at her. A soft chuckle escaped his lips when it bounced off her forehead. "I was only messing with you. But I need to head out now. Can you finish this up yourself?"

She stood, relieved. "You had me going there, Stephen. I thought for sure I'd made you angry or something. Thanks for the help."

"Thank *you* for allowing me to assist."

"As if I could stop you." She rolled her eyes.

He grinned. "You mentioned baking last night."

"Yes. I baked cookies. There's a plate covered in tinfoil on the counter for you."

He gave her a lopsided grin and a wave. "I'll grab it on my way out."

One look at the clock had Bailey rushing to her room. She needed to get ready for church. Although she hadn't planned to decorate this morning, she'd enjoyed Stephen's company. He was a difficult man to read, but he actually seemed to enjoy spending time with her. Her heart pattered a bit faster at the thought. Would he ever be able to see her for the person she was, or would he only see her as his mother's dowdy assistant?

After going home to change and grab his Bible, Stephen headed into Bend. He gripped the steering wheel so tight his hands hurt. What was going on with him? He wasn't himself. That much was clear.

And he really needed to stay away from Bailey so he could think straight. For whatever reason, she messed with his head—not her fault though. He didn't expect to be attracted to anyone, much less his mother's assistant, but he was drawn to the reserved woman. He pulled into a church parking lot. He'd never been here before but had heard good things from Bailey's client, Mrs. Gladstone.

His family had built this building, although he hadn't been involved with it since he'd been in France at the time. He recognized Rick's trademark craftsmanship. His brother had a gift with wood.

He pulled the door open and stepped into the space, immediately feeling at home. Earth-toned walls framed tile floors. His mother's touch was apparent, from the reclaimed wood feature wall to the lighting. Talk about being wired to notice details. He blocked out the design features and strolled into the sanctuary where worship music streamed through the speakers. A seat near the back appealed, and he sat.

A short time later, he noticed Bailey rush in wearing black slacks and a purple jacket. She slipped into a row a section over and focused on the screen above the stage. He stood with everyone else and joined in the worship, doing his best to block Bailey from his mind. He knew few of the songs since he'd been out of the country and many were new, but he enjoyed worshiping nonetheless.

His mind strayed to all that was going on with his family as the pastor dove into the book of Mark and spoke on giving thanks—fitting. Thankfulness didn't flow from him. Frankly he was uptight. Concerned with the changes he saw in his mother, afraid she was dying, irritated that he didn't quite fit into the family business anymore even if Rick said he could have his old position back, frustrated that everything had changed, and to top everything else off, Bailey's secret admirer was annoying him too.

Then again, the attention seemed to be good for her self-esteem, so he shouldn't be so bothered. But he was. He had no claim on her, but he had come to care about her almost as soon as they'd met, and he didn't want some mystery dude breaking her heart.

What was it that made Bailey doubt herself? She'd shined

that first day he'd helped her redecorate Mrs. Gladstone's house, but he'd noticed her insecurity from time to time. Especially when she was with his mother. Did Mom intimidate her? And what had Bailey so upset last night when he saw her through the glass door in the kitchen? She'd tried to hide it, but he'd seen her red-rimmed eyes. His heart went out to her, but he didn't know what he could do other than be her friend. It would be a fine line to balance between being her friend and her boss.

CHAPTER NINE

SUNDAY AFTERNOON BAILEY SCOOTED OUT OF her car and waved to Nicole and Sarah, waiting beside Nicole's Mini Cooper. Bailey's boots sank into the inch or so of fresh snow that covered the sidewalks. Good thing she'd worn sensible footwear today. The drive here had been uneventful, and best of all, she hadn't spotted the silver car. Maybe it had been a coincidence after all. She grinned and took in the quaint western-themed town. She'd never done her Christmas shopping in Sisters, Oregon, but she had high hopes of finding the perfect gift for each of the people on her list.

She strolled over to her friends. "I hope you weren't waiting long."

"We got here right before you." Nicole zipped up her white puffer jacket.

"Are you ready to shop?" She couldn't wait!

They looked at each other with looks she couldn't decipher.

Didn't they enjoy shopping? They'd been friends for over a year, but shopping had never come up. This adventure had been her idea. Had they come only out of politeness? "Is everything okay?"

"Yes," Nicole said. "We were hoping for lunch first. Neither of us took time to eat after church." Her friends went to a service in Sunriver, so they'd traveled farther than she had from Bend.

"Oh. Sorry. I didn't think about food, but now that you mention it, I could eat." Bailey wanted to get through her list today, since she'd be so busy in the coming weeks, but food was a good idea. "How about Sisters Coffee?" It was one of her favorite places to sit and relax.

"Perfect." Relief showed on Sarah's face. "They make good sandwiches and pastries."

Nicole led the way across the street toward the coffee shop. "It's busy."

Bailey wasn't the least bit surprised since this was a popular stopping place for travelers. Her parents had made a point to eat here every time they visited the area when she was a girl. She fell in love with the pastries at Sisters Coffee along with Central Oregon during those vacations. "I'm sure it won't take too long." Her stomach rumbled. "At least I hope not." Funny she hadn't even realized she was hungry before the idea of food was brought up.

They stepped inside the lodge-like shop. Rich aromas scented the warm air. A fire crackled in the grand stone fireplace off to their right, and the hum of voices welcomed them. This place felt like a big bear hug—warm and cozy.

Ten minutes later, they found a table being vacated not far from the stone fireplace and snagged it.

Bailey pulled her secret admirer's Christmas card from her purse and handed it to Nicole. "That showed up in Stephen's car the other day when we were shopping."

"What do you mean showed up?" Sarah asked.

"It appeared out of nowhere. I have no idea how it got there except that we saw Spencer at the tree lot and Spencer delivered flowers to me the other day. He says the flowers aren't from him. I'm inclined to believe him, but all the evidence points to him, so . . ."

Nicole pressed her lips together.

Bailey lowered her voice. "Do either of *you* think Spencer is my admirer?"

Sarah shook her head. "He's a no nonsense kind of guy, not a romantic. I don't see him having anything to do with something like that."

"And yet he delivered the flowers," Bailey said. "What do you think, Nicole? He's Mark's friend, so you know Spencer best."

"I'd have to agree, he's not a romantic. Then again, the man is full of surprises. He once loaned Mark and me his canoe on the spur of the moment."

"So you're saying it's possible he's my admirer?"

"I'm not saying anything." Nicole looked away.

Could her friend know something and wasn't saying? If that was the case, then she really had no reason to worry, but what if Nicole was actually concerned, but stayed quiet so Bailey wouldn't worry? What if the person leaving things for her was actually the silver-car person?

"Okay then, what's our plan for today?" Sarah asked. "My list is short." She sent a pointed look toward Nicole. "Should I tell her?"

Bailey looked from one woman to the other. Did this have something to do with her secret admirer or was there something else? Her stomach knotted, and the old phrase two's company, three's a crowd, ran through her mind.

Nicole nodded. "You can trust Bailey."

Curiosity threatened to override good sense, but Bailey pressed her lips tightly together. This wasn't about her, and she didn't want to make Sarah feel uncomfortable.

"I know. It's so embarrassing though." She sighed. "I'm a recovering shopaholic. It's a serious problem that's taken me a long time to overcome and to pay off the debt I accumulated. Now I try to only shop from a list, which I've kept short today so I don't get sucked back into my old ways. Christmastime is rough. So going from store to store might be problematic for me."

"Thank you for trusting me, Sarah. Maybe we can visit only a store or two and call it good?"

"That'll work." Relief shown on Sarah's face.

"My list is short too." Nicole pulled out her smartphone and opened to her notes. She flashed the list toward them. "I imagine it won't take long to make all of our purchases."

Bailey shifted in her seat. "My list is kind of long, but since I have my own car, the two of you can take off when you're ready." She'd been looking forward to this day, but understood Sarah had a problem, and she refused to be the cause of her falling into old habits.

"How is work going, Bailey? Nicole told me about your boss."

"It's been weird. Mona's in the hospital, and I'm running the business." For which she felt completely unqualified. "I'm supposed to hire an assistant, but I'm not getting any response to my ad. It's probably the time of year causing the problem, but I can't do it all alone. Even from her bed, Mona was a big help, but now she isn't doing anything." Forget the fact she felt so lacking half the time. What if she messed up and lost a job for the company? More than anything, shopping today was cathartic. She needed to stop worrying about work.

"What about her son?" Nicole asked. "I thought he was helping you. From what I hear, the two of you make a good team."

Who had her friend been talking to? "To a point, yes. But it's not like he's an interior designer. He doesn't draw up designs and meet with clients." But from what she heard, he could if needed. Apparently he was an architect with an eye for both interior and exterior design.

"He's the uncle to those kids we saw at Bachelor?" Sarah dug into her sandwich.

"Yes."

"He's good looking," Sarah covered her full mouth as she spoke. "I heard he's a widower."

"That's true." Bailey's face heated. She couldn't explain why, but talking about Stephen felt weird. Maybe it was because she'd never had a bunch of girlfriends who sat around chatting about boys when she was a teen. She gazed at the tall, skinny Christmas tree in the corner of the shop near the hearth, reminding her of Stephen and decorating the tree with him this morning. She'd enjoyed their time together. She shouldn't have had so much fun when Mona was laid up in the hospital.

Based on what Stephen said, this could be her boss's last Christmas. She owed a lot to Mona. The woman had believed in her enough to mentor her and turn over the business to her. If only she believed in herself. Unless . . . Did Mona really turn things over to her, or had Stephen done so out of desperation until he could find someone more suited to the job?

"What's wrong?" Nicole asked. "All of a sudden you look like you could be sick."

"I'm fine. Just letting my thoughts stray to an unpleasant 'what-if.'" She quickly ate the remainder of her sandwich and washed it down with the rest of her mocha. "Are you ready to shop?"

Her friends nodded.

Sarah pushed back from the table. "I already know what I'm getting everyone."

Nicole's eyes widened. "What?"

"Coffee beans from here. It's the perfect gift, and I won't be tempted by a bunch of stuff while browsing the other stores, since my list will be completed."

"You're going to get coffee for everyone on your list?" Bailey asked. She thought to purchase a nice selection for her parents but had other items in mind for everyone else.

Sarah nodded solemnly. "It's for the best. My family understands, and they are all coffee addicts, so this is perfect."

The lunch rush had dwindled so Bailey joined her, and in less than ten minutes she had her parents' gifts purchased.

"Now where should we go?" Nicole asked. "I want to get something special for Mark."

"I can't believe you're getting married on Christmas Eve." Sarah shook her head.

Bailey's eyes widened. "I didn't even think about the date being Christmas Eve. I'll be in Salem for Christmas." Disappointment washed over her.

"You *have* to come. We're having a very small wedding at our church in Sunriver with only a few friends."

The last thing Bailey wanted to do was disappoint her friend, but her family was counting on her. Maybe she could go to the wedding and drive home right after. She didn't like the idea of traveling on the pass at night, especially if the weather was bad, but her friend's wedding was important too. "Okay. If the weather cooperates, I'll be there."

Nicole grinned. "Thank you. Now what should I get for Mark?"

"I have no idea." She didn't care to admit she'd never had a boyfriend to buy a gift for. She guided them across the street to an art gallery. "This place has nice pieces. Maybe they'll have something that speaks to you."

"Art isn't really his thing." Nicole pointed toward another storefront. "But he enjoys reading." They meandered into the bookstore instead. Nicole found several books she wanted and decided on a couple she thought Mark would like, including a first edition by one of his favorite authors. "Okay. Now to shop for the girls on my list. Let's head to the main drag. I saw a place I want to check out."

They walked until they came to a women's clothing store and went inside. The place looked pricey, but that didn't deter Nicole or Sarah. They both quickly found several outfits to try on.

Sarah held up a solid black dress with classic lines. "This would look great on you, Bailey."

"I'm not shopping for me today."

Nicole waved a hand. "You never shop for you, and it's about time you freshened your wardrobe." She shot a conspiratorial look toward Sarah. "After all, you are the face of Belafonte Designs, and you need to look the part."

Bailey shriveled on the inside. Nicole had basically said what she'd known since she was a kid—she was lacking. "What do you suggest?" Her voice came out strangled sounding.

Nicole's brows scrunched. "Giving you a makeover isn't intended to be an insult. It's my Christmas gift to you. I know we let you think today was your idea, but Sarah and I have had this planned ever since we learned that you're taking over for Mona. Your suggestion to go shopping today worked in our favor." She handed her an envelope. "Merry Christmas! Open it."

Bailey looked from Nicole then to Sarah and back to Nicole. "You did this for me? Why?"

"Because we care about you. I don't know who made you feel like an ugly duckling, but you are a swan who needs to spread her beautiful wings."

Bailey blinked back tears. "You're a good friend." She hugged Nicole right in the middle of the clothing shop.

"Ah, you guys," Sarah dragged out the word. "Now I'm going to cry."

They all giggled like a bunch of schoolgirls.

Bailey opened the envelope and her eyes widened. *Five hundred dollars!* "This is too much! I can't accept." She held a pre-paid visa card out to Nicole. "You're a school teacher, and I know you can't afford this. Especially since you are planning a wedding."

"Don't you tell me what I can and can't afford. I'll never buy you another gift if it makes you happy, but you are going to accept this. I have the entire afternoon planned out. Including a hair appointment in Sunriver. Please, Bailey. Don't ruin our fun. Planning this day has been about the best present I've ever given myself."

"Given yourself?" Her friend made no sense.

"Yes. I've never been in a position to pamper anyone before, and for the first time in my life, I know what it means to give joyfully to not only the Lord, but to a friend. It was Sarah's idea to start with, but I ran with it. I know it's extravagant, but that's what makes this so much fun." Her pleading eyes were so sincere.

Bailey blinked away threatening tears. "Thank you. I accept your gift."

Nicole looked at her watch. "My hair stylist agreed to come in today just for you. We have two hours until your appointment, so we need to get a move on."

"But where did the money come from?"

Nicole got close to her ear. "Remember that scavenger hunt my grandma sent me on?"

She nodded.

"Well, she left me more than the house. When I say this isn't going to set me back, please believe me."

Bailey nodded. "I do. Thank you." She felt like a child in a candy store. "Where do I start?"

"With these." Sarah thrust several items into her arms.

Four hours later, Bailey stood in front of the mirror in her bedroom in shock. She'd done something she never imagined and had her hair relaxed so all the kinky curls were gone, then she had it cut short into a bob-like style that went to right above her chin.

It looked healthier than it ever had and perfectly framed her face. They'd stopped at a one-hour eyeglass store and had new glasses made with frames that made her look chic. The change was mind-blowing. How could a haircut and glasses make her feel and look so much different?

Her closet held a new pair of versatile black booties, two pair of jeans, three tops, and two fabulous dresses. She'd purchased the classic black dress from the shop in Sisters and loved how pretty it made her feel. Since Nicole's wedding was an evening affair, she planned to wear it there for the first time. For now, she wore an old pair of comfy sweats and a T-shirt. She needed to finish up the tree downstairs and then call it a day.

She padded down the stairs and paused at the bottom. Christmas music played softly. "Hello?" She followed the sound to the living room and found Stephen along with his niece and nephew finishing up the tree. "Hi there."

Lacy whirled around. "Wow!" She ran to Bailey and hugged her around the waist. "You look so pretty."

Bailey laughed. "I'm wearing sweats and a T-shirt." Her gaze smacked into Stephen's. Was that admiration in his eyes? All from a haircut and new glasses?

Lacy leaned her head back and looked up. "Your hair looks so soft and pretty. Can I touch it?" She stepped back.

Bailey started to laugh, then realized the child was serious. "Okay. I guess." She squatted down.

Lacy petted her hair as if she were a dog. "It's so soft. My mom is going to be jealous."

"I very much doubt your mom would ever be jealous of me. That's like Cinderella being jealous of her ugly stepsisters." The idea that Judy would care one whit about her hair almost made her laugh. "What are the three of you doing here? I didn't expect company." She raised a brow at Stephen. He'd promised not to use his key except in an emergency.

"I told Rick that I'd watch the kids for a couple of days. We ran out of things to do at my place, and I noticed you were gone all day." His eyes met hers and held. "Now we know what you were up to. You look amazing, although you looked good before too."

Lacy giggled and looked between them.

Bailey's face heated. She hadn't expected such a strong reaction, and she was even wearing sweats!

Stephen cleared his throat. "Anyway, I figured you hadn't had time to finish the tree. We were trying to be sneaky and finish it to surprise you. I hope you don't mind."

A spark shot through her, and her face warmed. "That was very sweet." Bailey patted Lacy's shoulder. "You are expert tree decorators. I think your grandmother will approve." She wasn't simply saying that to make the children happy. They'd done a decent job. She'd only need to move a few ornaments to spread them out a bit. It looked like the designer's eye was hereditary.

Lacy grinned up at her with admiration on her face. "I knew she would. We found your pictures of the tree from last year, and we're trying to copy it."

"Oh. So you cheated. And here I thought you were design savants." Bailey offered them a teasing smile.

Stephen ducked his head. "Guilty."

"We're spending the night at Uncle Stephen's," Collin said.

"How fun. But don't you have school tomorrow?" It seemed odd that Rick and Judy would allow their children to have a sleepover on a school night.

They nodded in unison.

She looked to Stephen for an explanation, but he remained silent and his face gave nothing away. "It seems everything is under control down here, so I'm heading to bed. Don't stay up too late. Your teachers won't like it if you fall asleep in class."

"We won't." Lacy ran to her and hugged her waist. "Good night."

"'Night, sweetie." She detoured into the kitchen for a glass of water, still pondering Rick and Judy's odd behavior.

"Short hair suits you."

She whirled around from her position at the sink. "Hey, Stephen. Thanks. My friends thought I needed a makeover since I'm taking over for Mona."

Pain etched on his face for a brief second, then his face smoothed. "About that. We need to talk."

CHAPTER TEN

Stephen stood in his mother's kitchen facing Bailey. She was truly stunning even in sweats. How did a simple haircut change a person so much? He studied her face a moment longer. He'd thought she was attractive before but now — wow.

"What's going on? Why do we need to talk about me taking over?" Bailey's voice wobbled.

"It's nothing bad." He wondered at the worry on her face. When would she trust him enough to not think the worst when he wanted to talk with her? He motioned toward a chair at the table. "I lined up a couple of interviews for this week. We need to get your assistant into place as soon as possible."

"I didn't know anyone replied to my ad."

"No one did. I contacted a school in Portland, and they put me in touch with two graduates living in the area."

"That was a good idea. I hadn't thought to reach out to the schools. My alma mater likely has a few recommendations too. I'll give them a call in the morning."

"Don't. Let's wait and see these candidates before we get anyone else's hopes up."

"Good idea." She fiddled with her hair and glanced toward the door.

"I like your new look. I liked the old one too, but this is nice."

"Thanks. My friends thought I needed an update." She touched her hair again. "It's been quite a day, and I'm beat. Will you please lock up when you leave?" She strode from the room.

He stood there staring at the empty space where she'd been only a moment ago. He couldn't figure her out. She was shy and timid about some things, and at other times she was bold. Like when he saw in her eyes she wasn't happy with him for letting himself and the kids into the house. Good thing the kids were with him, or who knows what would have happened. Not that he was afraid of a little verbal sparring, but he preferred to avoid it if possible.

"Uncle Stephen, we're finished," his nephew called.

Stephen sighed. "On my way." When Rick had told him things were not going well with Judy, he'd had no idea how bad the situation really was. Apparently Thanksgiving was a show for the family and the kids. They'd left after church for a couple's retreat. He thought it odd that it would be held during the week, and that either of them would take time off to go, but he was glad they were trying to work things out.

He and Rebecca had been opposites in almost every way, but that's what made them compatible. She had qualities in her that he lacked and admired and vice versa. Would he ever have that kind of relationship again? He hoped so.

Collin slid to a stop in his socks at the kitchen doorway. "What's taking you so long?"

"Sorry, buddy. I'm letting my mind wander. Let's go. Morning will come faster than any of us would like." He ruffled his nephew's hair as they strolled side by side to find Lacy.

She stood before the tree staring, seemingly mesmerized by the lights. Maybe Bailey had been right in saying the lights were the most important part.

"We're leaving, Lacy. Unplug the lights please." He waited for her to do as he asked, then they paraded out the door. He locked up and guided them along the lit pathway to his cabin.

Lacy looped her arm around his. "Are you ever going to give

us cousins, Uncle Stephen?"

His chest constricted. "That's quite a question for this time of night." It was only nine o'clock, but it wasn't a topic he cared to discuss. He and Rebecca had wanted children, but she couldn't have them. They'd tossed around the idea of adoption, then they'd found out she had stage-four melanoma, and seven months later she was gone.

"Oh. Okay." Lacy's shoulders slumped. "I thought—"

"You know I'm not married, sweetie."

"You could get married. Plus, lots of people have babies when they aren't married."

"True. But not me." Single parenting did not appeal in the slightest. He pushed open the door to his cabin. "Wash your face and brush your teeth, then I'll come and tuck you both in." The large guest room had bunk beds as well as a queen-size bed. The kids thought it was super fun to sleep in bunk beds. He eased onto the couch and rested his head back closing his eyes. The clock on the mantle ticked loudly in the quiet room.

Sudden bickering in the bathroom grabbed his attention. "Finish up. You have to a count of thirty to get into bed." He raised his voice a little louder and started counting slowly. His niece and nephew turned off the water then raced to the bedroom. "Twenty-eight, twenty-nine," he drew out the word as he stood and strode toward the guest room. "Thirty." He jumped into the room.

They giggled uncontrollably.

"Settle down now. It's time to say your prayers." He tucked them in and listened to them pray, then turned off the light and retreated to his own room.

First thing tomorrow, he'd set up interviews with the two people the college had connected him with regarding the position. Hopefully one of them would be a perfect fit. It was unlikely they'd have any contact with his mother, but if so, they'd need to keep what he was up to from her. If she knew that he not only disregarded her order to fire Bailey but instead promoted her, she'd have a conniption. Good thing he had the legal right to do as he thought best with the company. Regardless, it'd be best to keep his recent decisions away from his mother, at least for a bit longer.

Based on the makeover he'd seen this evening, Bailey seemed to be embracing the idea of taking over the business. He hadn't expected her to step up the way that she had, although he probably shouldn't be surprised. Mom would never have hired her if she hadn't seen something special in her. Now to make sure Bailey knew she had what it takes. The ugly stepsister comment she'd made earlier made him doubt she knew how attractive she was, sweat pants and all. Is that why she came across as insecure at times?

The following afternoon, Bailey carried two mugs of coffee into the home office where Stephen waited. She placed it on the desk that faced the French doors. A cozy seating area on her left drew her attention. "Perhaps it would be best to conduct the interview there." She waved toward the love seat and two occasional chairs.

Stephen stood. "Good thinking. It's a little casual, but perhaps the desk is too formal." He handed her a printout about the first candidate. "As you can see, Celia is well qualified."

She skimmed Celia's information. On paper the woman looked good, but her personality and references would be the clincher. "What about the other woman?"

He handed her another paper. "I like this one the best."

She glanced over the woman's qualifications and was impressed by her work history. More than likely she was in her early thirties. A more mature assistant might be nice. "Sierra — nice name."

The doorbell pealed.

Bailey placed the papers on a chair. "Be right back." She took several calming breaths before reaching the door and pulling it open. "You must be Celia. I'm Bailey."

The fresh-faced woman nodded. "This place is really something! I'm stoked to be here." She held out her hand. "It's nice to meet you."

"You too." Bailey guided the eager young woman to the office. Fifteen minutes later the interview was over, and Bailey sat beside Stephen. "Was it me or was she like a mini-tornado? I'm exhausted."

He chuckled. "She certainly was excited or maybe overly nervous."

Bailey twisted to face him. "She's not the one. I don't think she and I would work well together."

"Agreed. It's weird how on paper she appeared perfect, but in person, not so much."

"No kidding. How'd it go with the kids last night?"

"Great. And I got them to school on time too, which was no easy feat. They'll be spending tonight with me also."

"Wow. In all the time I've been working here, Judy and Rick have never been away overnight without their kids."

"They needed some alone time together. And I've thoroughly enjoyed the kids. I feel like they grew up so much in the time I was away." He rubbed his chin. "I shouldn't admit this, but I have no idea how old they are anymore."

Somehow that didn't surprise her. "Collin is seven and Lacy is ten."

The doorbell rang, and Stephen stood. "I'll get it this time."

Bailey quickly checked her reflection in the full-length mirror behind the closet door. She'd never been one to worry about her appearance, but Nicole's concern that she look the part for her new position had struck a chord with her. Because she wasn't a beauty didn't mean she couldn't be pulled together. Her black slacks and red cowl neck sweater were perfect to her way of thinking. Certainly not corporate America, but it looked nice and was comfortable.

A petite woman of indiscernible age with blonde hair and vivid green eyes glided into the room.

Bailey stood and held out her hand. "I'm Bailey Calderwood. Thanks for coming to meet with us on such short notice, Sierra."

"It was no problem." Sierra settled onto the love seat. "Mr. Belafonte tells me that I would be your assistant if I get the job. What would be my responsibilities?"

Bailey explained what she needed and was surprised to see the disappointment in the woman's eyes. "Is there a problem, Ms. Robbins?"

"No. I had hoped this position would have something to do with interior design, but I'm sure I will learn a lot watching you."

"Thank you. I like your attitude. There is definitely room for growth in this position." She glanced toward Stephen. What if she'd misspoken?

He gave a nod of approval. "I agree. We are in transition right now, but as things settle, I could see your responsibilities expanding."

Bailey sat quietly while Stephen asked Sierra several questions then lounged back and propped a foot on his knee. "I like you, and I think you'd make a nice addition to Belafonte Designs." He looked to Bailey.

"I agree." A good thing too! She'd thought they would

discuss this privately before offering her the job, but there was no doubt this woman was more than qualified and appeared to be easy to get along with.

Stephen rose and offered his hand to Sierra. "Welcome to the Belafonte Design team."

Sierra stood and shook his hand. "Thank you. When do I start?"

They worked out the details, then Bailey walked her to the door. "I look forward to working with you, Sierra." It would have been nice if she could have started tomorrow, but she needed to give notice at her current place of employment. After Sierra left, Bailey turned to Stephen. "That was easier than I thought it'd be."

"Me too." He grinned then glanced at his watch. "Oh no! I'm very late. I was supposed to pick the kids up from school over an hour ago."

"I'm surprised no one called." Bailey pulled her cell phone off the desk. "Uh-oh. Nicole has been sending me texts about the kids, and I didn't notice." She responded to the last message.

The reply buzzed in. *With me. Need to leave soon. Hustle please.*

"My friend has the kids. She teaches third grade at the school. You met her on Thanksgiving Day at Bachelor. I'll go get them."

"I remember. Let's go together. I think we both need a breather."

She grabbed her stuff and an envelope fell to the floor. She quickly picked it up, then slipped on her coat and followed him to the door. "I can get them. It's not a problem."

"I understand, but I messed up, and you shouldn't be the one to face everyone's wrath."

"In that case, I'll stay here."

He shook his head and draped an arm across her shoulder. "Oh no you don't. I need moral support."

She laughed. The idea that this accomplished, sophisticated man had an iota of insecurity in him was preposterous, but apparently not impossible. "If you insist." She settled into Mona's car that Stephen was still using. The envelope with her name grabbed her attention. She'd never seen it before, so how did it get into her stuff? That was a mystery for later. She slit it open and pulled out a Christmas card with a snow scene on the front. She opened it and gasped. Stephen had said something similar last night. Could he be her admirer? She glanced his way.

"What's wrong?"

"Nothing. My admirer is growing bolder." She waved the card in the air like a fan.

"What did he say?"

She studied his profile. It had to be him. Stephen was the only person with access to her belongings. Surely he expected she'd figured out *he* was her admirer—at least she hoped he was because if not, someone who didn't belong there had been in the house. But that didn't explain Spencer delivering the flowers. *Hmm.* "It says, I think you're nice and pretty too." Okay, so it was a little amateurish, but he was a man. Not all men were poets.

"That's it?" His brow furrowed.

She flipped the card to the back. Had he added something there? "It appears so. I guess my admirer is a man of few words. What are you and the kids doing this evening?" She tucked the card into her coat pocket.

"I have no idea. Suggestions?" He pulled out of the driveway and pointed the car in the direction of Three Rivers Elementary.

At least it was a weekday and there wasn't much traffic. Weekend tourists going to and from Sunriver and Mount Bachelor slowed traffic. "How about takeout and a Christmas movie? Or if you don't mind stopping at the grocery store, I could cook. Or we could go out."

She wasn't sure how well behaved Collin was in public, so didn't want to risk a meal out with the seven-year-old. "I'm happy to cook."

"No. You're busy enough. Takeout is fine." He made a right at the light and a few minutes later they parked at the elementary school. "Lead the way. I have no idea where to go."

"Another reason you needed me along," She tossed over her shoulder as she strode ahead of him across the parking lot. Nicole was probably getting annoyed by now. Bailey would be if put in the same situation. They didn't have far to go. Nicole stood on the front porch of the school and waved. "The kids ran inside to use the restroom right before you got here."

Stephen stepped forward. "I'm really sorry about this. I was supposed to pick them up today, and I lost track of time."

Bailey rested a hand on his arm. "Stephen is watching his niece and nephew while their parents are away. I should have paid more attention to the time too. I'm really sorry, Nicole. But I promise to make it up to you."

"How?" She crossed her arms, but her eyes softened.

She had to think fast. "No matter what, I will be at your wedding."

Nicole's face split into a grin. "This was totally worth missing the cake in the teachers' lounge for. You promise you'll be there?"

"Absolutely!" Now she had to break the news to her parents. She would miss Christmas Eve. Hopefully they'd understand.

The drive to Sunriver Village was quiet. The kids sat sullenly, each looking out the side windows of the backseat still clearly upset they'd been forgotten. Even though it was only twenty degrees outside, ice cream was in order.

"I have an idea." She turned in her seat to face Collin and Lacy who sat with their arms crossed. "What if we get burgers and shakes?"

Collin caught his breath. "Really? Mom never lets us eat like that."

Stephen glanced her way. "It's a little early for dinner."

"I'm hungry enough to eat now," Collin said.

Lacy giggled. "We should do it. It'll be fun. Plus, when I'm drinking a chocolate shake I might forget how late you were."

"She's good," Bailey said softly.

Stephen cranked the wheel to the left and pulled into a parking spot. "An early dinner it is." They all piled out.

Bailey couldn't help smiling. This little girl had her uncle wrapped around her finger.

Lacy and Collin walked between them as they made their way to the Village Bar and Grill. Which was more like a family restaurant than a bar.

Stephen held the door open for them as they paraded inside. Warm air and the scent of burgers and fries enveloped them. Her stomach growled, reminding her she'd skipped lunch. Since the place wasn't busy this time of day, they were served quickly.

Collin bit into his cheeseburger. His eyes widened as he chewed. "This is de-lish! Thank you, Uncle Stephen."

"Yeah. Thanks!" Lacy reached for her milkshake and took a long draw from the straw. "I wish our mom and dad would bring us here."

"You've never been?" Bailey asked.

"We almost never go out to eat. Mom has a cook."

"Now why didn't I know that?" Stephen asked. "We could have used your cook."

Lacy shook her head. "Mom gave her time off."

"Oh. Our loss."

"Nah-uh," Collin said with a mouthful. "This is yummier. Our cook only makes vegetables and beans and tofu." He stuck a finger in his mouth like he was gagging himself.

Bailey chuckled. It sounded like Judy was a health nut. Thanksgiving must have been a letdown if they were accustomed to a professional chef and a vegetarian diet. Although, maybe the health kick was new since they all had quite the sweet tooth.

The kids gobbled down their meals, and she enjoyed her cheeseburger and fries as well. Bailey dabbed her mouth with her napkin. "That was so good."

Stephen nodded. "I agree." He leaned close to Bailey's ear. "Wanna go ice skating?"

Her heart kicked into double time. The last time she went ice-skating she'd broken her arm.

Stephen chuckled as Bailey gripped his arm. "You've skated before haven't you?"

"Once. And it didn't end well," Bailey said through gritted teeth.

"Sounds like a good story." He patted the hand that held tight to his arm. "I'm sure whatever happened was character building." That had not come out in the playful way he'd hoped. If only he could snatch the words back.

She grimaced. "Not so much. I ended up breaking my arm."

"Ouch. Sorry." Apparently she had some fear of the ice to deal with. "And now you're afraid you'll fall and break your arm again?" He eased them forward, and they glided side-by-side.

"Pretty much." Suddenly her feet slipped forward. She grabbed his arm with both hands and steadied herself.

His heart raced. "You okay?"

"I'm still standing." She offered him a wobbly smile.

"Way to be positive." He grinned. "I happen to be an expert

skater. I'll have you skating on your own in no time." That is, he would, if her ankles were strong enough. "You're going to have to let go of me for a second, so I can move to face you."

Her fingers plied off one by one until he could slide in front of her. He reached his arms forward and skated backward. Her ankles wobbled a little, but not too bad. "You're doing a good job, Bailey. I won't let you break your arm again."

"Promise?"

He chuckled. "I'll do my best."

Collin and Lacy glided past them, giggling the whole way.

What were those two up to? He glanced over his shoulder to make sure the way was clear as he guided Bailey around the small open-air-but-covered rink. "You having fun yet?"

She shook her head, even though a small smile tugged at her lips. "It's not so bad actually. I can do this."

"Good for you. But I think I'll stay close anyway." He released her hands and continued to skate backward watching her. Though a little wobbly, she was doing all right.

A boy jetted by clipping her skate. "Oh—" Her arms shot out, and she whirled around. There was nothing he could do to help. One foot crossed over the other as if in a slow motion axel. She screamed as her feet came out from under her, and she landed on her back. Her head smacked the ice.

His heart thundered as he crouched beside her. "Are you okay?"

CHAPTER ELEVEN

STEPHEN HANDED BAILEY AN ICE PACK. "How are you feeling?" He sat beside her at the kitchen table.

"Like a klutz." She held the ice pack to the back of her head. "I'm sorry for ruining things for you and the kids."

His heart melted. "Your wipeout wasn't entirely your fault. You had a little help. A kid clipped your skates when he was dodging someone else."

She winced. "I remember."

"I never should have encouraged you to skate after you said you couldn't." Come to think of it, she didn't ski either. Her ankle strength wasn't really the issue like he'd thought at first. She simply didn't have a good center of gravity when it came to slippery surfaces or people throwing her off balance. "Are you sure you're okay?"

"I'm fine. The doctor who was at the rink with his family even confirmed it. Stop worrying."

Not true. "He said you have a mild concussion." When she landed on her back smacking her head into the ice, his heart had nearly stopped.

The kids had been solemn on the ride home too, obviously concerned. They now silently looked at books in the other room. He didn't want to leave Bailey since the doctor had discretely told him to keep an eye on his wife. His heart had constricted at the doctor's words, but he hadn't corrected him.

It was an understandable mistake, especially since his niece and nephew strongly resembled the Belafonte side of the family. The faux pas that would have been gut-wrenching a year ago now only made him wince.

A hand on his arm brought him from his musings. His eyes met Bailey's. "What's wrong?"

"I was about to ask you the same thing."

He covered her hand with his, gave it a light squeeze, and stood. "I'm going to run the kids to John's."

"I thought they were camping out at your place tonight."

"Change of plans."

"I hope it's not on my account."

The sad look in her eyes made him want to pull her close and tell her everything would be okay, but that was crazy thinking—they barely knew one another. One would think he'd bumped his head too. Then again, they'd been spending a lot of time together. He stood and walked toward the passage that led to the living room. "I'll be back a little later to see how you're doing. I plan to use my key to let myself in."

"I guess that's fair warning, but I really am fine. You don't need to change any plans for me."

He shrugged. "This will make me feel better." He turned and marched into the living room. Maybe sending the kids to his brother's wasn't such a good idea after all. He lived in a studio apartment that was not fit for children. Maybe John could stay over at his place. It'd probably feel like a castle.

He made the call and was pleased when his brother agreed, although John was more than a little surprised to learn that Rick and Judy had left the kids with him. Didn't Rick tell John anything? Stephen was close to both his brothers, but John and Rick rarely saw eye to eye. Considering Stephen had been out of the country for so long, he'd expected his brothers would have bonded by now.

"Uncle John is coming to camp out with you kids tonight. He'll be at my house soon, so let's get over there."

Lacy and Collin looked at him with puppy dog eyes.

"What?"

"What about Bailey?" Lacy asked. "What if her head starts to hurt worse, and there is no one here to take care of her. Can she come too?"

He only had the one guest room, but it would be easy enough to work out sleeping arrangements. "I'll ask her."

"Ask me what?"

"The kids want you to join us at my place tonight."

She shook her head then winced. "I don't think so."

"Please," Collin and Lacy said in unison.

"All my stuff is here."

Stephen snapped his fingers in an ah-ha moment. "We'll stay here. There are plenty of rooms."

"No." The firm tone in her voice said it was a closed subject. He couldn't blame her. Having all of them here would create a lot of extra work for her, and according to the doctor, she was supposed to take it easy.

"You heard her. Let's scoot." He ushered the kids to the door then turned and mouthed *I'll be back*. He chuckled when she wrinkled her nose at him. The woman had no idea how cute she was. Cute or not, she was getting under his skin, and he wasn't sure how he felt about it.

Relief washed over Bailey when she finally had the house to herself. Nothing against Stephen and the kids, but her head hurt, and all she wanted was a hot shower and comfy clothes. Thirty minutes later, she sank onto the couch with her laptop and started making a list of the things she wanted Sierra to take over.

A rap sounded on the door and then the deadbolt turned over, clueing her in to Stephen's return. "In here," she called out.

A moment later he eased into the chair closest to her. "What a day!"

"Tell me about it. I'm glad we found my assistant. I'm working on a list of her duties."

"I heard once that you're not supposed to use a computer when you have a concussion."

"I'm fine."

He shook his head and gently removed the computer from her lap then placed it on the desk and brought her back a pen and pad of paper. "Please do it the old fashioned way for a few days. Let your head heal."

Touched by his concern, she nodded.

"Today has been so long, it feels like we hired Sierra days ago." He yawned. "John is staying over tonight. I thought I might crash in my old bedroom."

She grinned. "That's not necessary. Other than a slight headache, I have no repercussions from the ice show."

He laughed. "And what a show it was."

She tossed a pillow at him. "Be nice."

"I thought I was."

She rested the side of her head against the seat cushions. When she first met Stephen, she never imagined being relaxed in his company, but over the past several weeks they'd spent a lot of time together, and they had found an easy camaraderie. "Now that I have the design part of the business in hand, what are *you* going to do?" She studied his reaction through the slits in her eyes.

He leaned forward, resting his elbows on his knees. "*Do* you have everything under control? I had the impression you were feeling insecure about taking over."

"I suppose I was at first. But now that I've had time to think about it, I know I can take Mona's place and train someone to take mine."

A sad look settled on his face.

"I'm sorry, Stephen. That was incredibly insensitive of me."

"It is what it is. My mom's future is uncertain, and even if she was healthy, she should be able to relax and enjoy life, not spend her days working. It's time she handed the reins over to someone else. I'll oversee Belafonte Designs from here forward, but you're the face of the company. We'll plan to meet at least once a week to discuss what you are working on, or to just keep me apprised of how things are going."

"Okay." A tingle zipped through her. It was funny how in a matter of weeks she'd gone from being uncertain about Stephen to wanting to spend as much time as possible with him. What would happen once Sierra started? Would they still get to see one another? She sure hoped so.

"I'll be your assistant until Sierra starts."

Yes! But wouldn't it be weird for both of them? "That's not necessary." But oh so appreciated. And here she was worried about not seeing him enough.

"I think it is. There is too much work for one person. Especially a person with a slight concussion."

"But *you* can't be my assistant." He was the boss. How could he even consider being a lowly assistant?

"What? I'm not good enough for you?" A twinkle lit his eye.

"No. You're *too* good to work with me."

He frowned. "I know you must be teasing, but I've always been of the opinion even when someone teasingly says something they believe there is a degree of truth to the matter. Otherwise, they never would have thought of it."

She shrugged and stood. "Perhaps. I'll see you in the morning." She brushed past him.

Stephen reached out, taking Bailey's hand as she passed him. "Who hurt you?"

She stopped and faced him. "What are you talking about?" Confusion showed in her eyes.

He stood to be closer to her eye level. "Who told you that you aren't good enough? I'm right, aren't I? That's why you always make cracks about yourself."

Her face paled. "My head hurts. I'm going to sleep. Goodnight." She turned and marched up the stairs. A moment later, the sound of a door firmly shutting filled the quiet house.

Well, he'd done it now. Hopefully he hadn't alienated her. One thing was for certain, whether she'd admit it or not—someone had hurt Bailey and so badly that she clung to it like a badge.

Lord please heal her pain. He headed to his old bedroom and softly closed the door behind him. Tomorrow was a new day, and as Bailey's assistant, he would have plenty of time to try and figure her out.

Who was he kidding?

Figuring out a woman could take a lifetime!

CHAPTER TWELVE

THE NEXT DAY BAILEY WALKED INTO Mona's house and headed up the stairs. Stephen had stuck to her like glue today, and she needed time alone. It seemed the only place she'd have solitude was her bedroom.

The front door opened and closed behind her. "I can whip up some dinner," Stephen said.

She paused on the stairs, took a deep breath and let it out slowly before turning to face him. "That does not fall within your job description."

"It seems to me you do a lot of things that don't as well." He smiled smugly. "I'm going to fix dinner. I plan to eat in thirty minutes. If you're hungry, there will be enough for you to join me." He sauntered in the direction of the kitchen.

Bailey snapped her mouth closed and rushed to her room. Five minutes later, she'd changed from her pencil skirt and silk blouse into comfy jeans and a sweater. The added responsibility of taking over for Mona was exhausting, and to make matters worse, her head ached. She fell onto her bed and closed her eyes.

Stephen had been a huge help today, but she felt awful about him doing her bidding. She should be doing that for him. After all, he was technically her boss now. It was all too weird. She'd never had her own assistant, nor had she ever been the boss. Maybe she wasn't cut out for it.

Her cell rang. Keeping her eyes closed, she felt on the bed beside her and grasped her phone. "Hello?"

"Dinner's ready."

She sighed inwardly. "Thanks, Stephen. I'll be right there." She didn't have the heart to tell him she was too tired to eat. Besides, when would a man cook for her again? Maybe never. She sat up and headed down to the kitchen.

Christmas music played softly as she entered the space and only one light shined over the stove where Stephen stood. She sniffed the air. "Eggs?"

"Omelets. I took a chance and made you ham and cheese."

She couldn't help grinning. "That sounds perfect." There were few things more comforting than breakfast for dinner. She took the plate he handed her to the table and sat. "Why's it so dark in here?"

"I like to be able to look outside when I'm cooking. Since it's dark out that's the only way I can see. Would you like a light on?"

"No. Actually, this is nice."

He joined her and offered a blessing for their food. "I made decaf coffee too."

"Maybe later. Thanks."

He nodded. "Dig in. Breakfast is my specialty."

"Why's that?"

"My wife was not a morning person, so I always cooked breakfast. It seemed to get her day off to a better start."

"That was sweet."

He ducked his head and forked a bite into his mouth.

Was he blushing? It was hard to tell in the dim lighting, but she couldn't imagine Stephen getting embarrassed over something so minor. She loved how light reflected off the snow making it look so much brighter outside than normal. Suddenly energized, she pushed back from the table. "Thanks for the meal. Leave the dishes. I'll wash them when I get back."

"You're leaving?"

"For a walk. I love strolling through the snow."

He stood. "I'll come too."

She paused. "You don't have to." Why was Stephen being so nice to her? The cards and flowers popped into her mind—that would explain his behavior, but why would a man like Stephen be interested in someone like her when he could have anyone? It stretched her imagination to fully believe he was her secret admirer, but the other options were not nearly as pleasant. At least she hadn't seen the silver car for the past couple of days.

"I'll walk as far as my cabin."

So he hadn't meant to walk with her after all. Disappointment hit her. What was wrong with her? One minute she didn't want his company, and now she was sad because he wasn't coming along to spend time with her, but was only heading to his place. She shook her head.

"Something wrong?"

Her eyes widened. "Nope. I need to grab a jacket." She rushed to retrieve her coat and boots.

Stephen stood at the door, waiting. "That was fast."

"Yep." She swept past him and out the door.

A moment later his stride matched hers as they headed along the path toward his cabin. "I thought our first day working together went well."

"Second," she said.

"Excuse me?"

"This is your second day playing my assistant. The first day was when you helped me at Mrs. Gladstone's house."

"That's right. Okay, second."

"You're very good at knowing what I want done even before I ask. How is that?"

"I used to tag along with my mom when I was a kid."

"Ah. So you've been apprenticed." No wonder he had an eye

for interior design. "I'm surprised *you* didn't take over for Mona."

The snow danced in the illumination of his front porch. "That wouldn't have been very smart of me. Besides, I have my sights set on something different. I'd like to start designing houses again."

"I wondered why you weren't drawing up plans for your family business."

He shrugged. "Timing is everything. I trust that once you get settled, I'll be able to follow my passion. After all, you've been working by my mom's side for the past two years so you know the ins and outs of the business. It shouldn't take you long to feel comfortable being in charge of the design branch. I have complete confidence in you."

"But still . . . You might do a better job." She pressed her lips closed. Why had she voiced her thoughts? It was like she had a broken filter where Stephen was concerned.

He stopped and turned toward her. "I wish you'd tell me what happened to cause you to doubt yourself, Bailey."

Stepping past him, she ignored his question.

He grasped her arm and drew her to a stop. "I'm serious. Why do you deflect compliments and knock yourself every time I praise your work?"

She pressed her lips together. What should she say? She looked over her shoulder in the direction of Mona's house. "I don't know. I guess it makes me feel uncomfortable."

"Why?"

She shuffled from side to side, suddenly cold.

He sighed. "Will you come inside for a few minutes while I start a fire? I'd really like to understand."

But I don't want to talk. How could she say no though? She nodded and trod beside him to the door of his cabin. "I don't think this is a good idea."

"Why? You afraid?"

She frowned. "Maybe."

"You don't have to tell me, Bailey. I only want to understand what's going on in your head. It'd be a lot easier to work together if we understood each other."

"Well . . . when you put it like that. Okay." She followed him inside, deposited her coat in the closet, and left her boots beside the door.

"Have a seat. It won't take long to get this place warmed up."

It actually felt pretty good in here after being out in the snow. She sat on the couch facing the fireplace.

He crumpled an old newspaper, tossed it into the fireplace, then added kindling and a few small logs. He brushed his hands together and stood.

Wood snapped and crackled as the fire took off. Stephen eased into the chair catty corner to the couch. "So . . ."

"Right. I really don't understand what the problem is. It's obvious that you would be the perfect replacement for your mom."

"Why?"

"Because I . . . I . . ." This was so awkward. She glanced over her shoulder toward the door. She'd give anything for a do-over tonight and skip dinner and conversation altogether.

"You what?" he asked gently as he moved from the chair to the couch.

"I don't know. You tell me."

He shook his head. "It doesn't work like that."

She cleared her thickening throat. "Fine. When I was a kid, I overheard a conversation that made a great impact on my life."

"Go on."

She took in a deep breath and let it out slowly. "I was at a sleepover with my cousin and a few friends. I left the bedroom for a few minutes, and when I came back, I overheard my cousin say that I was ugly, along with some other hurtful things."

"She was probably jealous of you."

"Her friends all agreed with her. From that day forward I knew the truth. I'm ugly."

"That's a lie. You are an attractive woman." He shifted closer and placed a hand on her shoulder.

She tilted her head toward him. "I know you're trying to be nice, but please don't patronize me. My mother does that, and I really don't appreciate it."

"Wow." He removed his hand. "They really messed with your head."

She looked away. "Well, now you know." She stood and turned toward the door.

Stephen darted around the couch. "Don't go yet." He stood in front of her, blocking her way and staring at her for a long moment. "I want to tell you, in all honesty, what I see when I look at you."

Her stomach fluttered. Why was he pushing this? Could he be serious? Did he really think she was attractive?

"I see a woman who tries to blend in but can't because she was created to shine. I see a woman with a keen eye for design, who could probably win one of those design shows on television, if only she believed in herself."

Her throat thickened. Those things couldn't be true. But why would Stephen lie? She shook her head. "Stop, Stephen. I—"

He touched a finger to her lips. "Shh. I'm not finished."

She gulped. Tingles zipped through her.

"Why did you listen to your cousin and not your mom?"

"Because my mom *has* to tell me I'm beautiful. She's my mom." She didn't want him to feel sorry for her or feel obligated to lie to her too, but if it had only been her cousins and friends she would have eventually gotten over their hurtful words. But time and again others confirmed their assessment of her. Maybe not in so many words, but when she was passed up when choosing teams or not invited to a party, she knew the real reason.

"I'm not your mom or your cousin, so I hope you'll listen to me. You're stunning, and your designs are as well. My mother knew a good thing when she saw you. Sure, you might have tried to hide your beauty in the past, but it's there for anyone who's looking to see. And your gentle spirit adds to your beauty."

"You think I'm stunning?" How could this be true? She shook her head in disbelief. Sure he'd complimented her before, but this time was different. She could tell from his eyes and the tone of his husky voice he meant every word.

He touched a hand to her cheek. "Yes, I do, and I really want to kiss you right now."

Her heart leapt and before she could respond, his warm lips gently touched hers. She stepped back. What had she done? This could ruin everything! "I need to go. Thank you for being so nice to me, Stephen." She rushed to the door, slipped into her boots and coat, and jogged all the way back to Mona's house. She burst into the kitchen then quickly locked up before parking herself on the floor in front of the lit Christmas tree.

Tonight had not gone the way she'd expected. All she'd wanted was a stroll in the snow but instead, Stephen said things she'd longed to hear. And kissed her in a way no one had ever done before. His kiss was oh-so-perfect and left her wanting more. But could there ever be more between them. He was, after all, her boss.

The lights on the tree blurred. She closed her eyes and rested her head on the seat cushion of the chair she leaned against.

"Lord, who do I believe? All the voices from my past or Stephen?"

Me. I love you and you are Mine.

Stephen stood at the picture window of his cabin looking out into the woods. Light snow cascaded to the ground adding a fresh coating, filling in his and Bailey's footprints. Today had been interesting to say the least.

Watching Bailey interact with clients and shopkeepers had been eye opening. He would have thought his mother's aggressive personality would be more desirable when dealing with customers, but Bailey's gentle approach seemed to work as well as his mom's methods, and in some cases, better. People didn't feel threatened by her but strove to embrace her vision.

A knock on his door drew his attention. Odd, he hadn't noticed anyone outside. He walked to the door and pulled it open. "Rick! Come in. What's going on?"

His brother stepped inside, slipped off his boots, and immediately parked himself on the couch in front of the fireplace. "I wanted to thank you in person for watching the kids."

Stephen sat in the chair beside the couch. "It was no problem. They were fun." If the tension flowing from his brother was any indication, something was up, and it wasn't good.

Rick frowned.

Unease gripped Stephen's gut.

"The kids told me that they spent a lot of time with you and Bailey. Is there something I should know?"

That was *not* what he'd expected to hear. "Oh. No. I don't think so. What do you mean?"

"I mean are you interested in her?"

"I am. Why are you asking?"

"Bailey is an important part of our business, and I don't want to lose her."

Rick didn't make sense. Unless . . . "*You're* not in love with her, are you? I know you and Judy are going through a rough patch, but—"

"Don't be absurd! Bailey? Come on, Stephen. You're as bad as my wife."

"What's that supposed to mean? You act as if there's something wrong with her. And what does Judy have to do with this?" Were he a dog, his hackles would definitely be standing on end. Where did his brother get off talking like that about Bailey?

"Nothing. And there's nothing wrong with Bailey. She's a great designer, but Mom would not approve of the two of you. Her health is bad enough without you breaking the news that you're falling for her assistant. You know how Mom feels about mixing business with pleasure."

Stephen shook his head. "Where is this coming from?"

Rick shot him a look that said little to ease his dismay with his older brother. What was really going on between Rick and Judy? And why did his brother care about his relationship with Bailey? He crossed his arms and narrowed his eyes.

"Mom is not doing well, and if you and Bailey started dating, I think she could take a turn for the worse."

"Do you realize how ridiculous you sound?"

Rick shrugged. "Think about it, little brother." He stood. "I need to go. Judy will wonder what's keeping me. But you'd better consider the consequences of a relationship with Bailey before things go any further."

"There's nothing going on." Well maybe there was a little more than nothing considering he'd kissed her a short time ago, but he hadn't had time to sort out his feelings yet—he was definitely drawn to her.

"According to my kids there is."

CHAPTER THIRTEEN

BAILEY SPOKE IN SOFT TONES TO Sierra, explaining what she expected of her. "Does all of that make sense?"

Sierra pushed a strand of blonde hair away from her face. "Yes. I think so. I know you said I wouldn't be designing right away, but to be honest, I'd hoped you changed your mind." Disappointment dulled her green eyes.

Bailey understood her assistant's desire, but she decided to train Sierra the exact same way Mona had trained her, even if Sierra was a little older than one would expect to be as a beginner in the design industry. Bailey would start her with little things that anyone could do, involve her in the process with clients, and gradually give her more and more responsibility. "In time, you will be given the opportunity to design, but for now, this is what I need from you."

Sierra nodded. "I understand. I didn't mean to sound ungrateful."

"Not at all." Bailey glanced toward Stephen who nodded approvingly from his corner of the office at Mona's house. "Now if you'll run these to this address." She handed Sierra a sticky note with the address of Rick's current project. "Rick Belafonte is expecting you, and he needs these tiles right away. When you're done grab lunch and meet me here afterwards." She pointed to the address at the bottom of the sticky note. "We'll be consulting with a new client and taking measurements."

Sierra's face lit. "Really? After what you said, I didn't expect to meet with a client on my first day."

In truth, Bailey hadn't expected to include her, but she was a softie. Plus, once Mona had started to include her in client consultations, it helped her grow as a designer and understand the business so much better.

Sierra stood and hoisted two boxes of tile into her arms.

Stephen rose. "I'll help you get these to your car." He muscled the three remaining boxes. "Is this it, Bailey?"

"Yes. Thanks." She rushed ahead of them opening doors. Once they had the boxes loaded, Sierra waved and drove off.

Grinning, Stephen sauntered over to her.

"What?" Her heart beat a rapid staccato. They hadn't spoken since he'd kissed her.

"You did a good job. And it was nice of you to include Sierra in a consultation on her first day. My mother never would have, but I like your approach."

She warmed from head to toe under his approving gaze. "Thanks."

He draped an arm across her shoulders and accompanied her inside. "I'll leave you ladies to your consultation this afternoon. It looks to me like you have everything well in hand."

"I should hope so." She chuckled. "Now that I think about it, other than needing approval from Mona on everything, I've been pretty much running the business." She frowned. "Do I need to come to you for approval on designs?"

He shook his head. "Remember, you are in charge now. Like I said the other day, we'll meet at least once a week to review all that's going on. Otherwise, I'll leave you to your job, and I'll start mine."

Her stomach dropped. "You have another job?" What about them? Shouldn't they talk about last night? Did the kiss mean nothing to him? She dared to hope they were becoming a couple, but she lacked experience when it came to men, so maybe she'd read the kiss wrong. They still stood right inside the doorway.

"Not officially, at least in the capacity I'd like. I'm going to do some research and draw up a series of designs for my brothers. If they don't want them, I'll sell them. In addition to my official job in France, I've been working freelance for a couple of years. There's no reason why I can't continue."

"I'm happy for you, Stephen. It's always nice to see someone pursue their passion." Maybe he had too much on his mind to think about starting a relationship.

"Back at you. Are you and I okay? You ran off so fast last night."

"Sure. No worries here."

"Good. Thanks." He strode along the path that cut through the woods to his cabin.

The quiet house suddenly felt lonely. She shook off the feeling and marched into the office. There was no time to dwell on her emotions. She picked up her briefcase, stuffed her laptop inside along with a measuring tape, then grabbed several product samples she planned to present to the homeowner this afternoon based on their brief conversation.

She sent a text off to Nicole to make sure her friend was still able to meet and to get her coffee order. She'd pick up their drinks and then go visit with her friend at the school. Nicole wanted to talk about her doing a presentation on interior design. Bailey couldn't imagine why anyone in the fourth grade would care one whit about what she did, but she owed it to Nicole to hear her out.

Thirty minutes later, Bailey strolled into the teachers' lounge with Nicole by her side.

"Thanks for meeting me here." Nicole pulled a salad from an insulated bag. "Did you bring lunch?"

"No. This peppermint mocha has enough sugar and calories

to count as lunch and dessert."

Nicole nodded. "Good point. I'm glad I had you get me plain coffee with cream and sugar." She pried the lid off her salad. "By the way, you look amazing. I noticed you are spending a little more time on your makeup too."

"Thanks. I don't want to let Stephen, or for that matter, Mona, down. They've been good to me, and I want to represent them well."

"You are certainly succeeding." Nicole ginned. "How's it going with the new girl?"

"Today was her first day. I wasn't expecting her to start for another week-and-a-half, but when her boss found out she was quitting, he told her he didn't need her and to enjoy her new job."

"Ouch. That sounds a little rude."

"I thought so too, but Sierra didn't mind, and I'm happy to have her start early. That will give me time to get her trained before Christmas."

"Have you been busy? I wouldn't think there'd be much business around the holidays."

"It's slower than other times of the year, but there's enough to keep us both busy since we also work on the construction sites."

"Cool. So, about visiting my classroom . . ."

"Right. I don't see how the kids could possibly be interested in anything I'd have to say."

"I disagree. I have several artistic students in my classroom. We are studying careers until winter break, and you'd be perfect. Plus, I happen to know the kids will love you even if you talk about something boring."

She chuckled. "When you put it like that, I can't say no." True or not, she owed Nicole after the makeover. She looked around then lowered her voice. "I was hoping you'd help me sort something out."

"If I can." Concern filled Nicole's eyes.

"I have a secret admirer."

Nicole grinned. "Mm-hmm."

"Well, I'm thinking it's Stephen, but I'm not sure because there have been some other instances that make me think it could be someone else."

"What makes you think that?" Nicole's brow furrowed.

Bailey told her about the cards and the flowers. "The flowers confuse me. It makes no sense to have Spencer deliver them. Especially since they don't really know one another. Then there's the fact that Stephen kissed me."

Her eyes widened. "He did? So are the two of you seeing each other or what?"

"Or what." She shrugged. "I have no idea what we're doing."

A bell rang. "I want to hear more, but I need to go get my class from the playground. Call me later if you can. I'll email the details for your presentation on Friday."

Bailey followed her friend as far as the end of the hall, then veered toward the office where she would sign out. A young girl sat in the office near the principal's door. Bailey hesitated for a second when she saw the child's face, which resembled her cousin's at that age so much they could be related. Her stomach knotted as the memories of that slumber party once again flooded her. She shook off the dread and quickly signed out, ignoring the girl.

Stephen sat at his drafting table in his cabin staring at a blank page. He'd been so excited about presenting his brothers with new designs, but now everything he thought of seemed boring.

He wanted to try something bold. Cutting edge. Something homebuyers would wonder how they had ever lived without. But nothing he thought of was good enough.

Knocking drew his attention. A quick glance at the window showed the sun had gone down. He wasn't expecting anyone, but he strode to the door and pulled it open. "Bailey! This is a surprise." He opened it wider. "Come in."

She shook her head. "I made stew and thought you might be hungry." She thrust a pot mostly wrapped in a dishtowel toward him.

"Thank you. That was nice. Please come in and tell me how it went with Sierra today."

"Are you sure? I don't want to interrupt anything." From her position right outside the door, she glanced around his cabin. Her eyes stopped at his drafting table. "That's new." She stepped inside.

He closed the door. "I moved it out of my bedroom. I prefer to work out here."

"Can I see what you've done?"

Stephen shook his head as he strode to the table. "I wish I had something to show you."

"You've done nothing? All afternoon?"

He laughed drily at the incredulous tone of her voice. "Trust me. I'm as shocked as you. I don't know what's wrong. I usually have tons of ideas flying through my head." He unwrapped the pot and lifted the lid. Steam surged up along with the savory smell of root vegetables and seasonings. "This smells delicious. When did you have time to cook?"

"It's been in the crock pot all day."

"I'm surprised I didn't smell it this morning." He pulled two bowls from the cupboard. "Will you join me? There's plenty."

"Sure. I left the rest in the crockpot on warm and haven't

eaten yet. Sorry. I didn't think to buy any bread."

"No problem." He dished up the stew then pulled out a chair for her. After he blessed the food he took a bite. "So how did it go with Sierra?"

"She's a quick study. If she continues to work hard and pay close attention to detail, she'll be a huge asset."

He studied her face. Although they'd known one another a short time, he was beginning to know her looks. He recognized concern, or perhaps it was worry, in her eyes. Maybe that was why she was really here this evening. "Penny for your thoughts."

"Not sure they're worth that much."

"Try me."

"I'm supposed to be the guest speaker in Nicole's classroom on Friday, and I'm not so sure it's a good idea."

"Why's that? Other than the whole public speaking thing."

She stuffed a huge bite of stew into her mouth and chewed very slowly.

He chuckled at her obvious avoidance of his question. "Fine. Don't answer." He devoured the rest of the stew. He hadn't realized he was hungry until he'd smelled her creation.

Bailey studied the contents of her bowl and finally met his gaze. "I'm scared."

"Of what?"

"What if the kids hate me and make faces at me, or talk over me, or—"

"Stop." He scooted his chair closer to her and cradled her hand in his. "Where is this coming from?"

She looked away from him. "There was a girl in the office today that was the spitting image of my cousin when we were kids, and it reminded me of that night and how it made me feel."

He ran his thumb gently across the top of her hand. "Ah, Bailey. That's your fear talking. Those kids are going to love you.

Just like Lacy and Collin do. You're great with kids, so relax."

Her cheeks flushed. "Thanks. I know I'm being silly. Old habits are difficult to break."

"Very true." He removed his hands from hers and stood, collecting their bowls. "I have peppermint ice cream. Would you like a scoop?"

"Of course. That's my favorite this time of year."

He pulled the tub from the freezer and took his time. His brother's stern warning hit him like a bucket of ice water. He really enjoyed Bailey's company and wondered if there could be more than friendship between them, but he never should have kissed her last night. His mother would not approve, and he strongly believed in honoring his mother—after all it was one of the Ten Commandments. He scooped up the ice cream then turned to find that Bailey was no longer at the table. "Bailey?"

"In here."

He followed the sound of her voice and found her on the backside of the Christmas tree. "What are you doing?" he asked as he handed her the dessert.

She took the dish. "Thanks. I wanted to see this side too. Your tree turned out nice. I didn't notice it last night though."

He grinned and walked toward the couch. "It was right there."

She followed him to the couch and sat. "I figured as much." She crossed one leg over the other. "I was thinking. Wouldn't it be fun if you joined me in Nicole's class on Friday?"

He nearly spat out his ice cream. "Why?"

"Two designers are better than one." She slid a spoonful of ice cream into her mouth.

"I don't know about that." Did she need the moral support? Of course, that had to be it. "On second thought, it could be fun, and maybe I'll be inspired. Count me in. Email me the details."

She grinned wide. "Thanks! I really didn't think you'd go for it."

"I'm full of surprises."

"That you are." The look in her eyes revealed something he hadn't noticed before. Bailey had a playful side to her. A side he wanted to explore. If only his family wasn't an issue. He didn't want to do anything that would put a permanent divide between him and Rick or his mom.

CHAPTER FOURTEEN

Friday afternoon, Bailey walked through the woods toward Stephen's cabin. The talk in Nicole's class could not have gone better. She wanted to celebrate, and Stephen was the closest person around since she'd given Sierra the afternoon off.

Squeals of delight met her ears as she neared the cabin. She grinned. It sounded like Lacy and Collin were visiting again. She'd sure seen a lot more of the children now that Stephen was home. Over the past six months or so, she had brought them back to the house several times when Judy was detained, but Judy seemed to be busy a lot more than usual lately. The strange thing was, when they did come face-to-face, Judy was cool toward her. Had she done or said something to offend Judy?

A snowball whizzed past Bailey's shoulder. She jumped and caught her breath. Before she could run for cover, another one smacked her thigh. She looked around for the culprit. Her insides leapt at the look of mischief on Stephen's face. "Was that you?" she called out.

"Don't you wish you knew?" He winked then ducked behind a wall of snow.

Smack.

She got hit from behind this time. Whirling around, she spotted Lacy run behind a pine tree. Bailey charged across the open space toward a juniper tree. She'd wandered into a war field. She ducked and formed several balls. The unusually wet snow soaked through her mittens as she packed it tight. A snowball broke near her feet. She stepped from behind the bush and pelted one toward Stephen. The snowball splattered on impact as it hit the wall of snow.

"That's the best you have?" Stephen hollered.

More giggling erupted. Suddenly the kids burst from their hiding places and high stepped it to where she crouched. "We can get him." Collin quickly made several snowballs then pelted one toward Stephen. "Take that!"

Bailey laughed. "I'm glad you're on my side."

Lacy giggled. "Uncle Stephen is the best!" She sneezed.

Bailey rested a hand on the child's shoulder. "Maybe you should take a break and go warm up inside."

"I'm fine." Lacy sneezed again. "Actually, hot chocolate does sound good." She stood and waved her arms. "I surrender. I'm not playing anymore." She tromped toward the cabin as best she could in the knee-high snow.

"I want hot chocolate too!" Collin went after his sister, sinking to his thighs in spots, but kept trudging along as fast as he could.

Bailey stood and came out from behind the juniper. "Looks like the game is over. The kids want to warm up inside." She hiked through the open expanse between the woods and the cabin.

Stephen met her in the middle. "You look like you could use a warm up as well."

Her teeth chattered. "I think you're right." She hadn't dressed in enough layers to be playing in the snow. She'd only planned to walk the semi-short distance between the two houses.

He draped an arm across her shoulder and pulled her closer as they walked side-by-side the rest of the way. "What brings you by?" he asked as they climbed the steps to his porch. He pushed the door open.

Warmth wrapped its soothing arms around her as she stepped inside. "I wanted to celebrate how well it went at the school today."

He grinned as he tugged off his gloves then shrugged out of his ski jacket. "That was actually fun. To be honest, I thought it could turn out to be a disaster, but the kids really responded well with good questions."

"I agree." She slid out of her boots and hung her coat on the closet doorknob, then dropped her wet mittens near the fireplace. Hopefully they'd dry quickly. "I know kids change their minds many times about what they want to be when they grow up, but one little girl told me she planned to be an interior designer." Bailey hadn't expected to have such a positive response to her talk. "Who knows, maybe someday she'll be my competition."

"It's possible." He sauntered toward the kitchen.

She followed on his heels. The kids were standing at the microwave heating water for hot chocolate.

"Do you have marshmallows, Uncle Stephen?" Collin asked.

"Do *I* have marshmallows?" He pulled open a cupboard and brought out two bags—one filled with mini, the other regular sized. "What's your pleasure?"

Collin pointed to the minis.

Thirty minutes later, a sharp rap on the door interrupted a game of Uno. The door swung open, and Rick stepped inside. His eyes widened when they met Bailey's. "This looks cozy."

"Daddy!" The kids shouted in unison and charged to their dad.

Bailey had the distinct impression that Rick's comment was not meant to be complimentary. He shot Stephen a look that seemed to be filled with disapproval. But what could Rick disapprove of? The kids were happy, safe and well cared for. The man should be saying thank you rather than whatever it was he was doing.

She stood and picked up her mittens from the floor. They were still wet, but at least they had dried some. "I should be going too."

Stephen eased from his seat and rested a hand on her shoulder. "Don't go yet." He stared squarely at his brother.

What was going on here? She felt like she was standing in the middle of a draw in an old western. Rick had always been great to work with, and she liked him. Why was he sending a vibe of disapproval her way?

"Get your things, kids. Mom is waiting in the car."

Lacy and Collin donned their winter wear then shrugged on their backpacks. "Goodbye, Uncle Stephen, 'bye Bailey," Lacy said.

Rick nodded at them then followed after his kids.

"What was *that* about?" Bailey stepped away from Stephen and crossed her arms.

"Nothing."

"That was way more than nothing. Rick looked annoyed. What's going on?"

"Don't worry about my brother. Remember I told you that he and Judy are going through a rough patch?"

She nodded. If she didn't know better, she'd think Rick was put out that she'd been at Stephen's, which made no sense. But what else could be the problem? It couldn't be the children.

"Unfortunately, he and I are going through a rough patch as well. Don't let him get to you."

"Oh." Maybe she'd misread the situation. Although she was happy the man wasn't upset with her, she felt bad he was unhappy with Stephen. "Is there anything I can do to help? I know there've been some issues at the current house he's building. Maybe I should—"

He held up a hand. "Relax, Bailey. You keep doing your job, and don't worry about my brother. I'll deal with him."

"Well . . ." She frowned. "I guess if you say so, I'll have to trust you."

A tender look covered his face, and he reached for her hand. "Thank you. I know things have been out of sorts for a while with my family, and I appreciate you sticking by us."

"Of course." Why did she have the feeling that he meant more than what he was saying?

Stephen had all he could do to keep from pulling Bailey into his arms. The confusion in her eyes followed by complete trust endeared her to him more than he imagined possible. But he needed to tread carefully. His family didn't approve, and he didn't want to hurt Bailey. Too much was at stake—first and foremost their hearts. What he needed was an ally, and he knew the perfect person for the job—John.

Bailey slipped her hand free. "Are you okay? You looked far away a moment ago."

He rubbed the back of his neck. "Yeah. I'm fine. My thoughts wandered. Sorry about that. Do you have any plans for this evening?"

"Nothing important. Why?"

He shrugged. "Thought we could hang out. Dinner. A movie. I have several Christmas movies in my collection, and I always keep a couple of pizzas in the freezer."

"How can I pass that up?" She grinned.

A jolt shot through him. "Great. I'll turn on the oven." While he was in the kitchen, he sent John a text asking to meet up with him the next day.

Bailey wandered into the kitchen holding several Blu-rays. "What are you in the mood for—comedy, classics, or a cartoon?"

"How about all three. *A Charlie Brown Christmas* is in there somewhere."

She pulled it from the stack. "Yep. That sounds like a winner to me."

They chatted for a while until the timer for the pizza buzzed. Stephen placed the pizza on a platter between them on the couch, then handed Bailey a plate. "Bon appétit." He downed a couple of slices then draped an arm across the back of the couch. Bailey sat at the other end with her feet tucked to the side and leaned against the arm of the couch. She looked so cuddly. He wished she'd sat closer to him. He'd been tempted to plop down beside her, but instead followed her lead and left space between them. Would she welcome his attention in that way, or would it make things awkward? His kiss had chased her away, but she'd come back, so maybe . . .

He would need to tread carefully. The business needed her, and he was beginning to realize that he did too. But why did his mom and Rick disapprove of her so strongly?

Maybe it was time he spoke with his mother regarding Bailey and get to the bottom of things before he drove himself mad trying to read his family's minds.

He glanced toward Bailey and froze. "What? Why are you looking at me like that?"

She reached for the remote that sat between them in the middle of the couch and pressed pause. "You had such a faraway look on your face—you seemed very sad or perplexed. I can't decide which. Are you okay?"

His heartbeat accelerated. "I'm fine. Just lost in thought."

"About what?"

He opened his mouth. Hesitated. He couldn't—not yet. "Family stuff."

"If you need someone to talk to, I've been told I'm a good listener."

"Nice to know, but I'm good. Thanks."

Her brows dipped. "Okay." She yawned and stretched like a cat. "Since you're not into this, I think I'll head to the house. I have a full day tomorrow and should get to sleep early."

"It's Friday night. What are you doing tomorrow?"

"For your information, I often work on Saturdays. But Sarah is throwing Nicole a bridal shower tomorrow, and I'm helping her."

He nodded, stood, and offered her his hand. "I'll walk with you."

"No need." She took it and allowed him to pull her to standing. "Thanks."

They stood so close. He should take a step back but instead gazed at the gold flecks twinkling in her hazel eyes.

She lowered her lashes and stepped to the side. "I'm not looking forward to the brisk walk. There's no need for you to get cold again. Why not stay here, and I'll text you when I get inside."

He shook his head. "No. I'll come. I need to stretch my legs anyway." Her suggestion made the most sense, but he didn't feel like being logical. He slid into his jacket and slipped a small flashlight into his pocket, just in case.

Bailey suited up for the cold too. "You really don't need to walk with me."

"I know." Didn't she want his company? Or was this her insecurity talking again? He pulled the door open for her and closed it behind them. Before she could get a step ahead of him, he grasped her bare hand with his. "Where are your mittens?"

"My pocket. They're still wet."

"No worries. I'll keep this hand warm."

A perplexed look crossed her face, but she remained silent as they strolled through the woods.

If only he could explain how he felt about her and why he'd backed off a little, but until he understood completely himself, he'd have to stay quiet. They came to the kitchen door and stopped. A light inside shone through the window, illumining the porch. "The kids had fun earlier," Stephen said.

She chuckled. "I think their uncle did as well. I know I did." Small snowflakes fell around them. She looked to the sky. "It's snowing again." One landed on the tip of her nose and another on her eyelash.

"Lovely."

She smiled. "I agree."

"No. I meant you."

"Me?"

"Yes, you. In case you haven't figured it out yet, I really like you, and I think you're beautiful." Forget his mother and brother. She needed to know how he felt.

"It's the makeover."

"No. You were beautiful before that. Your sweet spirit shines through in everything you say and do, only adding to the beauty already there. I would really like to take you out sometime." He'd sort things out with his family later.

"On a date?" Her voice squeaked.

His heart hammered. Had he read her wrong? "Yes. Preferably someplace warm."

She chuckled. "Like coffee?"

"That sounds perfect. Your friend lives in Sunriver, right?"

She nodded.

"We could get coffee after her shower tomorrow if you don't already have plans."

"Umm . . . Sure. I'd like that. How about we meet at *Brewed Awakenings* at four o'clock?"

He couldn't help the smile that tugged at his lips. "I'll see you then."

CHAPTER FIFTEEN

Bailey fidgeted in her seat and glanced toward the window as Nicole opened a slinky nightie from Sarah. If only she wasn't the kind of person who liked to save the wrapping paper. At this rate they'd be here all day! The family room was filled with so many of Nicole's friends from work and church that several ladies sat on the floor.

Sarah leaned close, keeping her voice low. "What's going on? You seem nervous or something."

"I'm fine, but this is taking a long time, and I have a date." The silver car was back. It'd followed her to Nicole's but kept going. She was officially freaked out. There was no way the same car would coincidentally be behind her so often. In fact, she was pretty certain she'd spotted it at the school yesterday too. She needed to tell someone. Nicole's fiancé was a cop, but with their wedding so close, she hated to bother them. Maybe she could talk to Spencer about it.

Sarah raised a brow. "You can cut out early if you need to."

"We'll see." She liked Stephen a lot. But confusion wracked her brain. He seemed to return her feelings, yet she had the impression from Mona that her sons, namely John, since he had been the only single one around for the past couple of years, were off limits.

Her stomach knotted. Maybe she'd accepted Stephen's invitation too hastily. She loved her job, especially now that she was in charge. Would a date with Stephen ruin that? Then again, it was only coffee.

Nicole finally opened the last gift and passed the long, white robe around for everyone to admire. "This was so much fun. Thank you! You're all the best."

A few minutes later, guests began to stand and gather their belongings. Within thirty minutes, Sarah's place was empty of everyone but the three of them.

"Thank you for throwing the shower."

"You're welcome," Bailey and Sarah said in unison.

Bailey checked her watch. Three-thirty. If they hurried and finished the cleaning, she'd make it. "Can I help you carry stuff to your car?"

"Yes. I could use an extra set of arms. That was a great turnout. I never expected so many people to actually show up."

Sarah nodded. "Clearly you're loved."

Nicole shook her head as if she couldn't believe it and wiped away a tear.

"What's this about?" Bailey asked.

"Before I came to Sunriver, the only person in my life who truly cared about me was my grandmother. My friends stopped coming around, and I suspect they never noticed I'd moved away."

"Why?" Bailey couldn't imagine how this lovely person might have ever been alone in the world.

"I used to be a workaholic with little time for anyone or anything other than caring for my grandmother or work. My students, lesson plans, and Grams were my life."

"Well, considering she had cancer it makes sense that you'd focus your energy on her," Sarah said.

"I know, but I'd shut out everyone else even before that. And now I feel so blessed to have friends again. I *never* imagined my life could be so full after that dark time. This place and the people

I've met here have really changed me. I'm a much different person than I was when I first came to Sunriver. And I'm very thankful."

Bailey had never seen her friend so serious. "I'm glad. And I'm happy I met the new you." She flashed a teasing grin. "But, I have a date, and I don't want to be late, so let's get a move on."

"A date?" Nicole's face lit. "Tell us more."

"It's only coffee."

"Who with?" Sarah asked.

"Stephen."

Nicole grasped her forearm. "You're kidding. When did this happen?"

"Last night. It's not a big deal."

"I thought you liked him. His niece and nephew sure think highly of you."

Her heart warmed at Nicole's words. "Thanks, and I feel the same about them and their uncle, but I'm not sure dating him is a good idea."

"Why not?" Sarah asked.

"Mona once told me her sons were off limits."

"But Mona's not in charge anymore. Right?" Nicole asked.

"True." She moved toward the door. "I have to go. If you want help, Nicole, unlock your car, and I'll drop off a load on my way to my car."

Nicole clicked the toggle on her key ring. "It's open. Thanks, and don't worry about Mona today. Just have fun."

Bailey nodded and grasped a bag filled with gifts on her way out the door.

Stephen sat at a large table in a small alcove. Talk about homey, and it would give them a little privacy. He was right on time but would wait to order until Bailey arrived. He let his gaze wander over the people in the room. One woman wore a candy cane striped Christmas sweater with bells tacked onto little green ribbons—talk about brave. She had a Christmas balloon bouquet on the chair beside her, which reminded him of Bailey's secret admirer.

She hadn't said much about him lately. Had he stopped sending cards and flowers? The whole thing troubled him. It wasn't like she had much of a social life, so who would be sending her things? The only person he could come up with was Spencer, but something about that didn't set right. Bailey said they weren't close. Maybe Spencer had other ideas?

He'd once thought he needed to walk a tightrope between being her boss and developing their friendship, but somewhere along the way, his feelings had shifted and he no longer cared for balance, especially if it meant opening the way for some other guy to date her.

The large glass door opened, and Bailey rushed inside. She looked around the dining area. Her face brightened when she spotted him. She waved and strolled over. "I hope you weren't waiting long."

"Only a few minutes."

Her pale pink sweater complimented her flushed checks. "Have you ordered?"

He shook his head. "I was waiting." He shrugged off his coat and placed it on a seat to save their spot. "After you." He motioned for her to precede him to the counter then placed their orders—two peppermint mochas. A few minutes later they carried their coffees back to the table. "How was the shower?"

"A huge success." Her smile lit her eyes as she took a sip. She placed the cup on the table. "So much so, I was afraid I'd have to cancel or be super late, but everyone cleared out fast. Sarah's house was packed with ladies."

"You could have held the shower at my mom's house."

Her mouth opened slightly before she clamped it shut and shook her head. "It never crossed my mind. Plus, we weren't expecting such a great turnout. A third of the women there didn't RSVP."

"Ouch. That must have been difficult."

"It was fine, but several people were sitting on the floor."

He chuckled. It served them right for being rude. However, he didn't care to talk about the shower. What he really wanted was to get to know Bailey outside of the job and find out if she had discovered the identity of her secret admirer. "I was thinking about your admirer while I was waiting for you. Has he come forward yet?"

She shot him a confused look. "Umm. No. Not exactly. What makes you ask?"

"Curious." The topic made her noticeably uncomfortable. He didn't want to ruin their date. "What do you do for fun?"

"Good question. Your mother has had me on a short leash for the past couple of years. Let me think." She sipped her mocha and stared out the window. Her face lit. "I love being outdoors. Nature inspires me."

"Me too." Didn't she do anything for fun? He already knew she couldn't ice skate or ski. "I enjoy many outdoor activities. Snow skiing, water skiing, kayaking, snowshoeing, rafting. You name it, I've done it."

"Rock climbing?"

"No. I haven't tried that yet." Although the famous Smith Rock wasn't far from there.

"So you plan to?"

"Probably not. I prefer to keep my feet on the ground."

She chuckled. "There's something we have in common. I also enjoy water sports, but it's been a long while since I've had time for any. I suppose I spend my free time chatting with friends or reading."

He could see that being the case. It was clear her friends were important to her, and in the very short time he was home, his mom gave Bailey very little time to herself. He only hoped Mom paid her well for all the hours she demanded. That was something he still needed to look into.

"Oh! I know. I like to shop. Granted, I mostly do so for work, but it gives me such a thrill to find the perfect light fixture or countertop or whatever. I think it's the challenge of the hunt that's so fun."

"So you're not a window shopper?"

She wrinkled her nose. "I've been known to, but it's not my favorite. I need a reason to be in the store. Mindless shopping is a waste of time, although I have found a few great buys when I've been window shopping."

Interesting. She was as driven as he was, but in her own way. No wonder she fit in so well with his family. He definitely needed to speak with his mother soon. He quizzed Bailey about herself and learned several things, including that she was an only child and that she grew up in Salem. She didn't fit the only child mold—at least not perfectly.

"What about you?" Bailey asked.

"I'm an open book. What don't you already know?"

She laughed. "If I knew that, then I wouldn't have to ask the question."

"First and foremost, I love the Lord. I saw you at church last Sunday."

She nodded with the hint of a smile.

"My family is important to me. I love living in the country.

I've wanted to be an architect since I was in middle school. I went to France to study the architecture and to work, but most of all to escape the memories here."

"But you're back now," she said softly.

He nodded. "I'm ready to move forward and stop running from the past. It will always be there, but I must move on. Rebecca would have wanted that for me. She would have liked you."

Bailey's eyes widened. "Why do you say that? From what I hear, we're complete opposites."

"In many ways you are, but she was as devoted to my mother as you are, and she cared as deeply about people as you do." He shrugged. "I think you would have gotten along well."

She nodded, evidently unsure what to think. Maybe he'd show mercy and give her a break from the subject. He nodded toward the exit. "You ready to go?"

"Yes." She grabbed her paper cup and stood. "This was fun."

"Yes. It was enlightening." He tossed his cup in the receptacle and held the door for her. "I'm headed to Bend to visit my mom. Maybe I'll see you later."

She nodded. "Say hi for me."

"Sure." They walked to the parking lot then parted company. He did not look forward to the conversation with his mother, but it was necessary.

CHAPTER SIXTEEN

STEPHEN RAPPED SOFTLY ON HIS MOTHER'S door at the hospital and waited a moment before entering.

"Stephen, come in and sit." Her coloring looked slightly better since he last visited.

He pulled the chair closer to her bed and eased into it. "I talked with your doctor, and he says you get to go home tomorrow." He'd put off finding a companion for her, but she would absolutely need care. Worry settled over him, but regardless of his concern he'd do his best to take care of her. "The doctor said no stairs, so I'll make up the guestroom for you in my house."

"I want to be at my own home in my own bed. You or one of your brothers can carry me to my room."

Her voice sounded stronger than it had, but concern for her health still made him rethink the conversation he'd planned to have. Then again, if they were sending her home, she must be well enough to have a difficult conversation. "Okay. That won't be a problem." But he'd have to move into the main house, which would not go over well with Bailey. Even if they *were* starting to date, he suspected she wouldn't want him living under the same roof.

"Good." She raised her chin and cocked her head to the side. "What brings you by? You look like you have something on your mind."

"You're right. In your absence, I've taken over running the

business."

Surprise lit her eyes for a moment before pride quickly replaced it. "Good. Was it terribly difficult finding someone to replace Bailey?"

He held back a sigh. He'd hoped to avoid this conversation, but he wouldn't lie to her. "No, because I didn't replace her. However, I did promote her, and I hired a talented woman with a lot of potential to be her assistant."

Mom gasped. "How dare you usurp my authority!"

He sat up in the chair and met her angry eyes. "With all due respect, I believe your illness has clouded your judgment. Bailey is exceptional at what she does. Sure, she's submissive toward you, but the more I think about it, I believe it is her way of showing you respect. I'd really appreciate it if you would trust me and let me deal with Bailey the way I think is best."

Her eyes had widened while he talked, then she suddenly rested her head back and closed her lids. "You're right, Stephen. Of all my boys, you're the most solid and intelligent." Her eyes narrowed. "If you repeat that to your brothers, I will deny I ever said it!"

He held in a chuckle. "Yes, Ma'am."

"I suppose I've been extra hard on Bailey." Her speech was still slow, but her words were becoming clearer, even after all her recent medical issues.

"Why?"

"It doesn't matter, but I'm pleased to hear you're happy with her."

His feelings for Bailey went way beyond that. There was so much he needed to tell his mom, but he wasn't sure now was the time.

"What else is on your mind, son?"

"How'd you know?"

"I'm your mother. It's not like you to sit there quietly and look so contemplative. You have something to say, so speak up before you miss your chance. You never know if this will be the last time we speak."

He winced. He didn't like it when she talked like that, but death was a part of life, which he needed to learn to accept whether he wanted to or not. "I have feelings for Bailey, and I'd like your blessing to pursue them."

Her eyes shot open. "Absolutely not! I'll concede that she is a good designer, and if you think she can represent Belafonte Designs at the standard that I expect, then okay, but I will not have her be a part of this family." Her voice shook, and she started to cough. Her pulse monitor beeped faster.

He stood and reached for the water bottle with a straw sticking out of it and held it to her lips. "I don't understand what the problem is." He kept his voice calm in spite of his aggravation. It would do no good to argue with his mother. He waited for her to finish then put the bottle back on the table on the other side of her bed within her reach.

"I'm too tired to discuss this further. Leave me. I'll see you tomorrow."

With a sigh, he took his mother's hand and gave it a gentle squeeze. "I love you, Mom. I will let this drop for now, but rest assured this conversation is not over." He left without a backward glance.

Time to get John's help. He sent a text to his brother and headed to his car. Maybe John could enlighten him about his mother's problem with Bailey.

After her coffee date with Stephen, Bailey set out to Bend to check on the house Rick was building. She needed to view the progress anyway. Halfway to the property, she noticed the silver car in her rearview mirror. "What is going on?" Using the hands free feature in her car she told her phone to call Spencer.

"Hey, Bails, what's up? It's not like you to call."

She quickly explained the situation.

"I'll notify the Sheriff and State Police and see if there are any deputies or officers in the area."

"What should I do?"

"You said this car has followed you to the building site before, right?"

"Yes."

"Keep going, but if there's no one there, don't stop. Instead go to the State Police office. Do you know where that's at?"

"Yes." Her palms sweated. "Are you sure about this, Spencer?"

"Yes. This person has never confronted you or made threats against you."

"There's a first time for everything."

"True. That's why you won't be getting out if no one is there. Stay on the line and talk with me until you arrive."

She did as he requested and even asked him about the Secret Santa. He denied being it, but indicated he knew who it was and that she had no reason to worry about who was sending her things. Well at least she didn't have to stress that.

She glanced in her rearview mirror as she signaled and turned off the highway. "He's following me off 97."

"Good. I was just notified that there is a State Trooper along the road up ahead."

"I see him."

"Good. Now drive normally. The trooper has been briefed

on the situation and will pull out after the silver car."

Sure enough, the trooper pulled out and a moment later flipped on his lights. She pulled up to the site and was only mildly surprised to see Rick's truck parked outside. She raced inside.

She knocked on the door then let herself in. "Hello! It's me, Bailey."

"In here!" Rick said.

Bailey walked toward the hall bath and spotted him hanging a mirror. "I didn't expect you to be here on a Saturday. I stopped in to check on the progress and make sure everything was moving along on schedule."

Rick finished what he was doing, then turned and looked past her as if he expected someone to be with her. "We got a little behind when I took off a couple of days. I'm working today to make up for it. The painters will be here on Monday to do some touchups, otherwise there is only finish work and landscaping left. Is Stephen with you?" He glanced past her.

"No. Are you expecting him?"

He shook his head. "The two of you have been spending a lot of time together, so I thought he might be. Excuse me."

She stepped aside, allowing him to walk past her. "Is everything okay?"

"Sure. Just busy." He strode down the hall then tromped up the stairs.

She followed after him. Why was Rick behaving so oddly? Regret hit her. She should have gone home rather than here. "Is there a problem, Rick?" She hated confrontation, but dancing around whatever was bothering him, especially when she felt like *she* was the problem, made her even more uncomfortable.

He stopped in the upstairs bath and began to mount the mirror to the wall. "You tell me?"

"What's that supposed to mean?"

Rick sighed, stopped what he was doing, then turned and faced her. "I'm sorry. Don't pay any attention to me. It's been a rough week, and I'm a grump."

Her eyes widened. "Oh. Okay. I'm going to take a few pictures then head out."

He grunted.

She wandered through the house taking pictures with her camera of all the high end touches—crown molding, medium oak hardwood flooring, stainless steel appliances, modern fixtures in the bathrooms, and a sliding barn door mounted on black hinges in the master that led to the walk in closet. It would be handy to have photos when she went to the warehouse to pick out merchandise to stage the place. Rick liked to stage their houses for a quick sale.

Satisfied she had all she needed, she tucked her phone into her purse and headed toward the door. Voices in the direction of the kitchen grabbed her attention. No one else should be here. She crept toward the voices, being careful to stay out of the line of sight, and listened.

"Lacy, when are we going to tell Bailey we're her secret admirer?"

Bailey gasped. The kids had sent her those cards and the flowers? Of course. No wonder Spencer said she didn't need to worry.

"Shh. She might hear you. Remember her car is out front."

"Sorry." He stage-whispered. "Do you think we made her feel loved?"

A tear slid down Bailey's face. She didn't know whether she was happy or sad. These kids were so sweet, but at the same time, her feelings were hurt that they all thought she was so unlovable.

"I'm sure she feels loved now, but we don't want her to know yet. Miss Nicole said it's good for her to think it's Uncle

Stephen."

Nicole is in on it too? She rushed quietly from the house, hoping the kids would be none the wiser. Rather than head back to Mona's, she would stay at her condo here in Bend. A little time to herself away from Stephen and the Belafontes sounded like a good idea.

She rushed out the front door and ran smack into Judy. "Oh excuse me. I wasn't watching where I was going." She blinked rapidly and swiped the tears off her face with the back of her hand.

"What do *you* have to cry about? Did my husband finally end his affair with you?" Hopefulness filled Judy's eyes.

"What affair?"

"Come on. Don't play dumb with me. I know what's going on. I've had a P.I. following you for weeks!"

"Does he happen to drive a silver car?"

"Yes. So?"

At least now she knew why the car had been following her, but how could Judy think her capable of such a thing? "I don't know what you think you know, but your husband and I are not involved in any way except professionally. I'm an interior designer and nothing more. Period."

Judy crossed her arms. "Prove it." Her voice held venom.

Bailey's pulse thrummed in her ears. How was she supposed to prove she wasn't having an affair? "Was your P.I. able to prove that I was?"

"Well, no," she sputtered. "But I know it's true."

"No, Judy." Rick's firm voice filled the silence. "I have been telling you for weeks that I am not having an affair with Bailey or anyone else. Let's take this outside. The kids are going to hear. If they haven't already."

"Fine," Judy snapped.

Rick closed the door behind them then faced his wife.

"Why are you never home?" Her voice hitched. "I came down here several weeks ago to surprise you, but when I saw Bailey come out of the house I stopped and talked to her. By the time I got inside, one of the guys said you'd gone to run an errand. I don't know how I missed you."

Bailey gasped. "I told you why I was here. I stopped in to deal with an emergency design decision after vandals ruined some cabinetry."

"And I left right away, to deal with something else." His face softened. "Is this what has come between us?" He blew out a breath. "Judy, honey. I love you more than anything, and I would never have an affair, much less with Bailey."

Ouch! She wouldn't go there either, but it still hurt the way he'd said it.

Judy's stance relaxed, and she stepped closer to her husband. "You're telling me the truth." It wasn't a question. "I'm so relieved. I know you've said it before, but I finally realize it's the truth." She wrapped her arms around Rick, then gasped and turned to face Bailey. "I've done something awful."

"What?" Rick asked.

"I told Mona that the two of you were having an affair." She looked sheepishly at her husband. "You've been so distracted since your mother's stroke. At first I thought it was because of your mom's health, and then I began to get suspicious that you were seeing someone. I kept seeing you with Bailey and well . . . my imagination took over."

Bailey groaned. "That's why Mona hates me."

Judy nodded. "I'm so sorry. I will tell her right away that I was wrong."

"Good." Rick placed a possessive arm across his wife's shoulder. "I'm sorry about all of this, Bailey. It seems my wife is more in tune with me than I realized. I have been up to something."

"Huh?" Judy asked.

His faced reddened. "I bought us tickets to go on a cruise, and I've been taking dancing lessons for the past couple of months."

Judy gasped. "Why so long?"

He frowned. "It turns out, I'm a really bad dancer."

Judy laughed.

Bailey took that moment to slip away and quickly went to her car. She sat inside and headed home for the first time in over a month. How could she have been so blind? All the little comments from Mona and Judy now made sense. Her face heated at what Mona and Judy believed her capable of. Absolutely crazy!

She definitely needed time and space away from the Belafontes. It was time to go home. She'd call Stephen and let him know her decision as soon as she got there.

CHAPTER SEVENTEEN

Sitting in his old bedroom at his childhood home, Stephen stared at the phone in his hand as if it held the answer to his problems. What was going on with Bailey? She couldn't have shocked him more if she'd told him she'd grown a second head since their coffee date this afternoon. What had caused her to leave?

"Stephen!"

"In here, John." He left his room. "Where are you?"

"Kitchen."

He roamed down the stairs and into the kitchen where he found his brother scavenging for food in the pantry. "I've been going to so many Christmas parties I'm 'sweeted' out. You have anything healthy here?"

"No idea. This is Bailey's domain." He pulled open the refrigerator. "How about eggs?"

"That works. Better than chocolate." John took the carton of eggs and whipped three in a bowl then scrambled them. "Do you want any?"

"No thanks." He had no appetite. "Mom is being released from the hospital."

His younger brother looked at him. "You're worried." It wasn't a question. "Why? Bailey will take care of her."

What was it with his family assuming Bailey would jump at their beck and call? "No. She won't. She's moving out."

John shut off the stove and pulled the pan off the burner.

"What did you do?" He looked half annoyed, half humored.

"Nothing! Why would you even ask that?"

He raised his hands. "Chill. I only meant to ask what caused her to move out. Where is she?"

"At her place in Bend."

John pulled a fork out and ate directly from the pan. "So was Mom's coming home and Bailey's moving out a coincidence?"

Stephen nodded. "It looks that way. But that's not even why I called you over here." He told him that Rick warned him against getting involved with Bailey and how their mom had reacted when he told her he had feelings for her.

"Whoa! How did I miss all this? You and Bailey? Man, I didn't see that coming. Our Bailey? Are you sure? She's not exactly your type."

Stephen crossed his arms. "What's that supposed to mean?"

"I don't know, just that she's not the kind of woman I see you with. So what is Mom's and Rick's problem?"

"That's just it. I don't know."

His brother devoured the rest of the scrambled eggs then rinsed the pan. "How does Bailey feel about you?"

He frowned. "I don't know that either."

John chuckled. "You're in quite a pickle. I've sure missed having you around. I didn't realize how much until now. I'm usually the problem child in this family."

Stephen wadded a hand towel and flung it at his brother.

"Hey." He laughed and set the towel on the counter. "I think you need to find out how she feels before you upset Mom."

"I wish I understood what the problem was there. Mom's objection makes no sense."

"You know Mom. She isn't always rational about things, especially when it comes to us."

"True." She once told him he couldn't date a girl because she didn't like her hair color. "But what about Rick?"

"He's a tough one. Honestly, I see no reason for him to object other than not wanting to upset Mom. Which, for the record, you shouldn't do."

"Great. Now you're against me too."

"Never. But we all know she's not going to recover from this," John said it as if it was a fact.

"She's coming home."

"Only because they can't do anything further for her. The infection must have cleared."

Stephen knew his brother might be right but wanted to believe she was coming home because she was improving. "It's been a long day. I'm going to bed. Lock up on your way out."

"Thought I'd crash here tonight and help you in the morning."

Tension rolled off Stephen's shoulders. "Thanks. 'Night." Having his brother here with him eased a huge burden.

The following morning a knock sounded on Stephen's bedroom door. He rolled over on his bed to face the door.

"Bailey's here picking up her stuff," John said.

He bolted upright. Of all days to oversleep. "Stall her?"

"How?"

"I don't know. Maybe offer to load her car with the stuff in the office that she wants to move, then go slow. I need time to take a quick shower."

"You'd better move fast."

Stephen darted to the shower and readied as fast as possible. He could hear his brother talking to someone. Good, she must still be here. He rushed out and nearly collided with Bailey.

"Easy there," she said.

He reached for the box. "I'll get that for you."

"Thanks." She brushed her hands together. "That went faster

than I expected. I thought I'd be here forever trying to get everything moved. All that's left are the flooring samples. I'll get them and meet you at my car."

"Sure." Standing in the driveway, talking in twenty-degree weather was not part of the plan. He took his time and sauntered slowly.

John gave him a silly grin and waggled his brows as he passed by on his way back inside. He always was the mature one—not.

He eased the box into the last open space in the trunk.

"Thanks for the help, Stephen." She laid the samples on the back seat. "I guess I'll see you Friday for our meeting."

That was it? "Actually, I thought I could follow you, help you unload, and then we could get breakfast before you go to church and I get my mom."

Surprise lit her eyes. "Really? You don't have to."

"I know. I want to."

"I'd like that. Thanks. I'll meet you at the office, and we can go from there. I only had a small amount of personal stuff, and it will keep until after church."

"You sure?"

"Yep."

An hour later, they were seated at a popular local restaurant. They were fortunate to be seated right away. He wiped his sweaty palms on his jeans. He ordered coffee for them then focused on the menu. He wasn't a coward, but yes, he was stalling.

"I've heard so many good things about this place, but I've never been. Have you?"

He nodded. It used to be a favorite. "You can't go wrong with their scones, and their omelets are exceptional." A moment later, their mugs were filled with coffee and their orders had been placed. "Anything more from that secret admirer of yours?"

She wrapped her hands around her mug and met his eyes. "Actually, I have two admirers."

"Two?" He raised a brow. How was he supposed to compete with that?

"Yes. Collin and Lacy." Her cheeks pinked. "They don't know I know, but I overheard them talking. I guess Nicole was in on it too, which explains Spencer's involvement. I can't believe I actually thought it was you." She gasped as her eyes widened.

"I wish I'd thought of it. But I've made no secret of how I feel about you. I hope you know, I really enjoy being with you. I'm going to miss having you next door."

Her eyes widened ever so slightly. He'd have missed her reaction, if he hadn't been watching so closely. "I'm going to miss you too. That's the only negative about moving back to my place."

"You sure I can't talk you into staying at the house?" He asked softly.

"There's a big part of me that wants to, but I feel strongly that this is the right thing to do."

"Because of my mom or because of me?" He leaned in.

"Neither. I need space."

"Why? Isn't my mom's house big enough for you?" His heart beat a rapid staccato. What wasn't she saying?

She shrugged.

"I suppose I can be kind of grouchy."

She laughed. "You're not grouchy. You are one of the kindest men I know. Your care and concern for your mother is admirable, and you step up to help your family whenever they need you." A smile lit her face. "Wait. I take it back. There was that one time."

"What one time?" He'd only been teasing about being grouchy.

"Right after your accident when you first arrived. You were a little grouchy that day."

He chuckled. "That day is a bit of a blur, but I do recall being kind of snappy."

She held her thumb and pointer finger close. "A smidge. To be perfectly honest, some stuff happened with Judy and Rick yesterday, and I need my personal space away from your family."

"And me?"

"No. Not you, but perhaps your mother."

"Fair enough. Will you tell me what happened?"

"No. You should talk to them."

"Okay." He took her hand. "I don't want to wait until Friday to see you. Can we get dinner together one night this week?"

"I'd like that."

It was time to have a serious talk with his mom.

Stephen couldn't wait another minute. He checked his watch for the umpteenth time—ten o'clock. Mom had slept late, but she should be alert enough to talk about Bailey now. He'd take her a cup of tea and toast to soften her up a bit.

He almost laughed at his ridiculous thoughts. He prepared a light meal and put it on a tray, then headed upstairs. "Knock. Knock," he said as he entered her bedroom. "Good morning, Mom."

"Hello, son."

He placed the tray beside her on the bed. "I've brought you a light breakfast."

"Thanks."

He helped her sit up.

She grasped the delicate teacup he'd used and sipped the tea. "You did a good job with this."

He grinned. "I'm glad you like it." He sat in a nearby chair and got right to the point. "I'd like to understand what your problem is with me pursuing a relationship with Bailey."

She choked on the tea and set the cup onto the saucer with a loud clatter.

"I see the question surprises you, but I really need to discuss this with you. I want to understand why you feel the way you do."

She said nothing and finished her meal in silence. Finally, she set the teacup down softly and cleared her throat. "I had believed something about her that turned out to be untrue. It pains me to admit it. I knew better than to think such a thing of Bailey, but I suppose I'm jealous of her."

Nothing would have shocked him more. He stayed quiet.

"She's young, with the rest of her life ahead of her. Her designs are fresh, and I see a bright future for her." She sighed. "The worst part is knowing that my career is over. I've built this business from the ground up. It's who I am . . . was. I'm a has-been."

"But not with me."

She patted his hand. "Thank you for that. What about Rebecca?"

"Mom, she's been gone nearly three years. I'm certain she wouldn't want me to be alone for the rest of my life. Besides that, I think Rebecca would approve."

"Why?" She looked more curious than confrontational.

"It's mostly a gut feeling, but Rebecca always rooted for the underdog, and if anyone is an underdog, it's Bailey. She's believed some outrageous lies about herself, which has set her on a path of self-doubt."

"I've noticed that too. But that girl overflows with talent."

"Have you ever told her?" He knew the answer before he

asked.

"Of course not. I wouldn't want her to get a big head."

"Do you really think Bailey is the kind of person to let a little affirmation go to her head?"

Mom's lips tightened into a thin line. "Perhaps not. But why take the chance?"

He shook his head. "You could make a positive difference in a hurting person's life rather than affirm the lies she's believed since childhood."

Mom harrumphed. "I'm tired. Please leave me now."

He stood, grasped the tray, and left. No! He refused to take this. He turned at the doorway and faced her. "Bailey has been so good to you."

"I'm not questioning that. I simply don't want the two of you to marry."

"Who said anything about marriage?" His voice rose a little, and he took a deep breath, then let it out slowly. Marriage. He hadn't thought that far ahead, but he could get on board with the idea where Bailey was concerned.

"I know you. We wouldn't be having this conversation if you didn't see yourself proposing to her at some point. But do what you want. I won't stop you." She mumbled something else that he missed.

He wanted to push her further, but her face had paled. It was time to let his mother rest. He went downstairs and found John reading the paper in the kitchen. "That didn't go well."

"I'm sorry. Should I try and talk with her?"

"No. She's resting. I thought we could bring her downstairs and settle her on the couch in the living room for a while so she could enjoy the tree and decorations."

"Good idea. I need to head to the office for a few hours. Do you need my help getting her down here?"

"No. She's as light as a feather. Will you come back when you're finished working? I'm sure I'll be ready to escape."

John chuckled. "I'll be here." He folded the paper then stood. "I am meeting with potential clients this morning. They're looking to build but don't want a cookie cutter house. I would like to show them your latest design."

A jolt shot through Stephen. Thankfully he'd finally come up with a new design plan. It wasn't much, but it was a start. "Thanks! Let me know how it goes."

"Will do." John grabbed his jacket and left.

Now what? Somehow he had to get his mother's blessing. He couldn't in good conscience continue to date Bailey without her approval. It would tear his family apart. *Lord please soften Mom's heart.*

CHAPTER EIGHTEEN

Bailey pushed her cart down the aisle at the grocery store. Getting to know Stephen had been fun, and she looked forward to knowing him even better, which was why she was strolling in the grocery store. She decided to invite him over for dinner rather than go out to a restaurant.

It had to be something easy and fast though. The meat counter grabbed her attention—stir-fry. She ordered a generous amount of the seasoned vegetable and chicken mix then finished shopping. Stephen would be at her place in an hour, and she wanted everything to be perfect.

Exactly one hour later, a knock sounded on her door. She looked around her place. The gas fireplace burned, creating a warm and cozy atmosphere. The white roses and greenery she'd picked up sat in a vase on the sideboard, and the table was set with plain white dishes on red placemats—simple elegance.

She pulled the door open and couldn't help the grin that captured her lips. He wore a hideous ugly Christmas sweater. "Hi, Stephen. Come in." She stepped aside allowing him to pass then closed the door. "Dinner is almost ready."

He breathed in deeply. "It smells great in here." He placed a kiss on her cheek. "You look beautiful." He handed her a bottle of chilled sparkling apple juice.

She took in his jeans and red sweater, hoping her face didn't match the color. He'd kissed her again! Well, her cheek. A part of her wished he'd shifted his aim ever so slightly and given her another real kiss. She cleared her throat. "Thanks. And you look very . . . festive."

He chuckled. "I know it's not exactly my style, but I spent the afternoon with the kids. I took them Christmas shopping."

"That's great! What's going on with your mom? How'd you get away?" She guided them back to the kitchen and opened the sparkling cider then poured them each a glass.

"John stayed with her this afternoon, so I could take the kids shopping. And the home care aide tends to her from six in the evening to six in the morning every day. Mom awakens early, so she is there to help ready her for the day. Oh, before I forget, Mom really liked the decorations."

"She saw them?" Bailey sipped the juice.

"Yes. I brought her downstairs for a couple of hours. I think it's good for her to be out of her bedroom."

"What a great idea." She flicked off the stove then dished up their plates. "I hope you like stir fry vegetables and chicken."

He nodded.

"Good." Relief surged through her as she brought the plates to the table. Her insides felt like they'd been stir-fried. Why was she so nervous? "Would you mind offering a blessing for the food?"

"Not at all." He took hold of her hand, closed his eyes, and said a short prayer. "I know I've already said it, but this really smells good. I've been eating a lot of breakfast food lately." He forked a bite into his mouth.

Bailey watched his face closely. Did he like it?

His lips turned up as he chewed, and he nodded. "Delicious."

"It's super easy. The meat department has it already prepared. All you have to do is cook it."

"What about the rice? That can be kind of tricky. Although I learned to cook in France, I'm not great at rice."

"Not if you follow the directions." She dug into her food in spite of her nervous stomach. He was right, it really was delicious.

"We need Christmas music." He looked around her dining room, presumably for something that played music.

She stood. "Sorry. I forgot how much you enjoy that. Hold on." She grabbed her phone off the counter and put on a mix of Christmas music she'd made. "How's the volume?"

"Perfect."

She returned to her seat. "Do you have plans for Christmas Eve?"

"Not really."

"As you know, Nicole's wedding is Saturday evening. I could really use a date."

He raised a brow. "You're asking me out?"

"I suppose so." Her heart pounded in her chest so hard she was certain if the music wasn't playing he'd hear it.

"I hate weddings, but in your case I'll make an exception."

"Thank you." She took another bite and chewed slowly before swallowing. "How can you hate weddings?"

He shrugged. "I have to wear a suit and tie, people cry, and to be honest they are kind of boring."

"Not all of them. I once attended a wedding where the bride skipped down the aisle to Chapel of Love. You know the one that says 'going to the chapel and . . .'"

He chuckled. "Now that would have been a fun wedding."

"It was. The bride and groom had a lot of fun." She shared a little more then realized she was talking about weddings way too much. What if he thought she was hinting at something? She almost choked on her food at the thought. She quickly finished up her meal and noted that Stephen had as well. She pushed back from the table. "I'll rinse these real quick."

"I'll help." He took his plate into the kitchen and worked by her side. "I have something I'd like to tell you."

A queasy feeling knotted her stomach again. "Okay. Should I sit?"

"Actually that's a good idea." He took her hand and pulled her along with him into the living room. He eased onto the sofa.

She sat beside him since he hadn't let go of her hand. "This sounds serious."

"It is to me." He released her hand and faced her. Tenderness filled his eyes. "I don't think this will come as a surprise to you, but I have grown to care deeply for you over the past four-and-a-half weeks." He reached up and cupped her cheek in his hand. His touch sent goose bumps though her. "And I believe you feel the same way. Please tell me I didn't read you wrong?" His eyes searched hers.

She rested a hand over his and swallowed back her fear. "I do." She'd *never* talked with a man like this before. In fact, she'd never had a boyfriend. She pulled her hand away and rested it in her lap.

"Good." He visibly relaxed then dropped a soft kiss on her lips.

Electricity shot through her. She wished his kiss had lingered.

"I'm meeting with some resistance to *us* from my family. Not all of them, but it's important to me that they welcome you into my life."

"They don't like me?" How had she misread all of them so badly? Or was this about Judy? Hadn't she set the record straight with Mona yet? She'd thought for sure Judy would tell her right away. Her throat thickened, and she blinked away sudden tears.

"Ah, Bailey. Come here." He pulled her close.

She rested her head against his chest. "I'm not usually a

crier." His heartbeat sounded faster than it ought against her ear.

"I'm handling this so badly." He sighed and kissed the top of her head. "The thing is, you're very important to the success of Belafonte Designs, and for the record, my niece and nephew adore you. Right now we need to be praying that God will soften my mom's heart. She admitted to being jealous of you."

Bailey pushed away from him. "Jealous of me? Why?"

"You're young, talented, and have the rest of your life ahead of you. You're filling her shoes in the business she created, and I think she's afraid you are going to take her place in the family too."

"That's absurd! I could never." She needed to talk with Mona right away and set things straight. She almost laughed at her thought. Confronting Mona or anyone else was such a foreign idea. Before she'd met Stephen, if anyone had told her she'd even consider confronting Mona, she'd have vehemently denied it. But she'd come to realize that she mattered, and it was important to live her life with purpose, rather than try and be invisible.

"You're quiet. What are you thinking?" He stroked the back of her hand with his thumb.

"That your mother and I need to talk. I need to make sure she knows the truth about something."

"You mean about Judy and Rick? They told me."

She nodded.

"I think she knows, but I also think we both need to be praying."

"For sure. Thank you for bringing this to my attention. I wouldn't want to disrespect your mother or come between the two of you or your family."

"You've surprised me."

"How so?"

"I didn't expect you'd want to deal with this."

She shrugged. "Some things—or people—are worth fighting for."

The following afternoon, Bailey sat in Mona's living room. Mona lounged on the couch, wrapped in a blanket, looking like she'd rather be anyplace but seated in the same room with Bailey.

"You did a fine job on the Christmas decorations."

"Thank you. Your grandkids and Stephen were a big help."

Mona's gaze shot to hers. "Love always makes things even better, don't you think?"

"Excuse me?" What was Mona getting at?

"When you do something in love the results are often, if not always, better."

"Oh. Yes. I believe you're correct." Could Stephen's mom be softening toward her? She'd prayed so much since saying goodbye to him last night.

"What brings you by, Bailey? I was told you moved everything back to the office."

"Yes. I'm actually here to see you. I tried to visit while you were in the hospital, but I was turned away."

Mona's lips stretched into a flat line.

"You see, I've come to care deeply about you and your family—Stephen in particular. I respect you, Mona." She took a calming breath. Her hands trembled, but she had to do this. "And I don't want to do anything that will upset you."

Mona's fierce look softened slightly. "Go on."

"I suppose that's all I really wanted to say. Other than thank you for being my mentor and allowing me to step in for you. I hope you are pleased with what you've accomplished."

"What *I've* accomplished?"

"My work is a direct result of your training. Sure, I went to school, but there's something to be said for one-on-one mentoring. Without you, I don't know where I'd be."

"True enough."

Although she didn't appreciate the comment, she could see Mona was considering her words. Had she said enough? *What do I do now Lord?*

Trust me.

Silence filled the room for several minutes. Bailey shifted to stand.

"Wait!"

Bailey stayed seated.

"I'm an old woman, and only the Lord knows if I will ever see you again. I need to say something." She licked her lips. "I pushed you hard, and I am not sorry for that. It's what made you the designer you are today. But I do apologize for being petty and for believing the worst about you when I knew you were not the kind of woman to have an affair. I was embarrassed that I needed your help so much, and I wanted to find fault with you. I'm a prideful woman. I need to work on that." A sparkle lit her eyes.

Bailey grinned.

"As for you and my son, I'd say he's met his match in you, young lady. I didn't realize it until now. You've taken me aback this afternoon, and I'm very impressed. Good for you!"

Bailey's insides leapt. "Thank you, Mona." She stood and approached the woman. "May I hug you?"

"I'm not a hugger. But I'll make an exception this one time." She opened her arms.

Bailey hugged the frail woman. "Merry Christmas. I hope you and I can be great friends someday."

Mona rested her hand over Bailey's. "Me too. I think we are

well on our way now that the air has been cleared. Merry Christmas, dear one. Promise me something."

"If I can."

"You'll take good care of my family when I pass."

"I wish you'd stop talking like that, but if they will have me, I will give them my best."

"Fair enough."

CHAPTER NINETEEN

BAILEY SAT NEAR THE FRONT OF the church in Sunriver with Stephen seated to her right. She still couldn't believe how things had turned out with Mona and the rest of the family. Only the Lord could have worked that kind of miracle.

Mark stood on the stage with Spencer, his best man, and the minister. All but the minister wore traditional black tuxedos. Sarah stood across from them wearing an off-the-shoulder, tea-length red dress. It seemed odd that Sarah would already be up there, but Nicole wasn't one to do something simply because it was expected.

A white cloth runner cascaded down the center aisle, and bows decorated the end of each pew. The stage had a lovely arbor decorated with twinkle lights. The flower arrangements had a Christmas theme and were made of holly, greenery and red and white roses. Soft classical music played over the sound system.

The music faded as a woman sat at the piano and began playing the Wedding March. Everyone stood and faced the center.

Nicole glided down the aisle solo, holding a simple bouquet of red roses. Her face glowed happiness. At the front, she handed her flowers off to Sarah.

They sat, and Stephen draped an arm across the pew behind her. She inched a little closer.

He spoke into her ear. "I have something to tell you."

"Now? The ceremony has started."

"You're right. It'll keep."

She wanted to dig an elbow into his ribs. All she could think about was what he had to say and missed several minutes of the ceremony.

What could Stephen want to tell her? She hadn't seen or heard from him since she'd been to the house this past week to visit Mona. In fact, she hadn't heard from any of the family. At least she knew things were right between them all now. It still bothered her a little that Judy thought she was having an affair with Rick, but she needed to get over that and move on since the rest of the family had.

She forced her focus onto Nicole and Mark as they said their vows. Maybe someday that would be her. Dare she hope Stephen would be the one she said her vows to?

"You may now kiss the bride."

She brought her focus back again and clapped as her friends sealed their marriage with a long kiss.

The pianist played *Joy to the World* as they walked down the aisle, and soon the guests were ushered out, row-by-row.

She turned to Stephen. "What did you think?"

"As weddings go, it wasn't bad. I like how simple and quick it was."

It sure was quick. Her mind only wandered off a little while, yet she missed half the wedding! They made their way to the reception line.

Nicole pulled her into a hug. "Thank you for coming. It means a lot that you are here."

"Your wedding was beautiful, and so are you."

Nicole giggled. Bailey grinned. *True love.* "I'm holding up the line." Not that it was overly long. When Nicole said it would be a small wedding, she had been serious.

"Okay, but be sure to stick around for when I throw the bouquet."

"I promise." She moved forward out of the way. The rest of the evening flew by in a blur.

A commotion near the exit drew her attention. It looked like Nicole was going to toss her bouquet. She left Stephen and headed in that direction. A flash of red flew over the heads of the single women who'd gathered and headed straight for Bailey. She reached out and grasped it.

A few people clapped, and Nicole looked as pleased as a child on Christmas morning. Her newly wedded friend turned and headed outside to a waiting sleigh. With a sigh, Bailey turned to look for Stephen. She didn't have to look long. He stood near the exit and motioned her to follow him. She slipped on her coat and rushed in his direction. "Are you ready to leave?"

He nodded. "But first I have a little surprise for you." He pointed to the parking lot where a second sleigh sat, complete with horse and a driver wearing a black top hat.

"Is that for us?" Her heart raced.

"Yes." He took her arm and guided her along the cleared walkway.

"How does the sleigh run on the pavement?"

"Wheels."

She chuckled. "Of course."

He assisted her in then draped a blanket across their laps. "I hope it's not too cold."

The driver made a sound and the horse pulled the sleigh forward.

"Not with you by my side." She hugged his arm and snuggled close. "Is this what you said you needed to tell me during the service?"

"No. I'd hoped to talk to your sooner, but you were quite the social butterfly tonight." He grinned. "We were in such a rush to get to the wedding that I didn't want to bring this up earlier, but then as we were sitting there, I realized I should have because staying quiet was torture."

"You certainly have my attention."

"My mom spoke to me this afternoon."

"About what?" She held her breath. Could Mona have told him about their conversation?

"She told me what a catch you are, and she gave us her blessing."

She let out her breath in a sigh of relief. "That's great news." She'd keep to herself that she already knew about Mona's change of heart.

"I agree."

"Now what?" She hated to show what a novice she was at the dating thing, but he might as well know sooner than later.

"This." He shifted then lowered his head slowly. A twinkle lit his eyes. He was only a breath away, then his mouth covered hers with a sweet kiss.

She closed her eyes as a tingle started in her toes and shot through her. She closed her eyes.

"Merry Christmas, Bailey."

She fluttered her eyes open. "Merry Christmas." It was the merriest for sure. She'd found her true love. A man who saw past her insecurities to the woman God made her to be. This was indeed a merry and blessed Christmas.

~The End~

A Note from the Author

Sunriver is a favorite destination for my family and me. I will never forget the year we went over the day after Christmas. Oh my goodness there was a lot of snow. My boys had a blast inner tubing on Mt. Bachelor. Because of this fond memory I wanted to include a scene at the mountain; however, it's my understanding from the woman I spoke with at the lift ticket counter, it's not always open for Thanksgiving since they need a good amount of snow, and that's still early in the season. But anything is possible in fiction.

Per my norm, I took a little creative license with the setting here and there, to make my story work.

I am pleased with the end result, and I hope you enjoy the story.

Kimberly loves connecting with her readers.
You may find her at:
www.kimberlyrjohnson.com
www.facebook.com/KimberlyRoseJohnson
Twitter @kimberlyrosejoh

You may also follow her on Amazon to be notified every time she has a new book release:
www.amazon.com/Kimberly-Rose-Johnson

A Sneak Peek at Book Three
in the Sunriver Series

CHAPTER ONE

SIERRA ROBBINS SAT IN HER SUV outside a mansion in Sunriver, Oregon. This was the last place she ever expected to live, but the timing couldn't be more perfect.

"Whoa! You're housesitting *here*?" her fifteen-year-old son asked.

She looked over at Trey and grinned. "Yes, and I expect you to treat this place like a museum. Don't touch anything."

He laughed. "Not likely, but I get it. I'll be careful not to break anything." He opened his door and stepped out. "What're you waiting for? Don't you want to see inside?"

"I've been inside. Remember? Mrs. Drake is a client." Unease gripped her. Not for the first time anxiety settled on her as she grabbed her purse. Did she make a mistake agreeing to house-sit? She took in the enormous house and pushed away her nervousness. There was no way living rent-free for a year could be a bad thing. They'd be living in luxury. Her son did online high school, so she didn't even need to worry about transporting him to and from Bend.

She pulled the key from her purse and marched up the wide concrete stairs leading to the front door. Trey took the stairs two at a time and stood waiting at the top for her. She tossed him the keys. "Remember don't touch *anything*! The art alone in this house could fund your college education."

"This place is amazing. Can I pick any room?" He asked as he wandered from one room into another.

"No. Mrs. Drake specifically said you could stay in the first floor guestroom off the entrance."

He popped his head around a corner. "Oh. Okay."

Sierra still stood in the grand entrance that opened onto a great room with a connected kitchen and dining room off-center to the left and a hall to the bedrooms on the right of the great room. The cool color scheme wasn't her favorite, but the home could easily grace the cover of a magazine. The heels of her boots clicked across the hardwood flooring as she made her way to the far wall of windows that faced the direction of Mount Bachelor. She opened the drapes and caught her breath. Although the ponderosa pines obscured the view, it really was breathtaking. It would be difficult to leave this place next spring.

"I'll get our bags." Trey breezed outside, and a moment later loud voices filled the air.

She ran to the door and froze. A police officer had his gun drawn on Trey who lay face down on the paved driveway. "What are you doing?" She shouted trying to keep her voice calm, but clearly failing.

He jerked his head toward her. "You're trespassing."

"No, we're not. I'm Sierra Robbins. Mrs. Drake told the security company that my son and I would be living here for the next twelve months."

He spoke into the radio on his shoulder, still keeping an eye on her with his gun leveled at her son.

Time ticked slowly as she waited for him to confirm her story. "You don't need to point that thing at him. He's not going to hurt you." She heard a muddled voice coming from his radio as he lowered his weapon and holstered it.

"Sorry about that, ma'am." He nudged Trey with his foot. "You can get up now."

Trey stood and glared at the cop.

Sierra rushed down the stairs on wobbly legs to her son's side and placed a hand on his shoulder. She'd love to wrap him in her arms, but he stood over a foot taller than she did.

"I'm Officer Preston." He offered his hand.

She took it, though begrudgingly. "This is my son Trey." Where did he get off pointing a gun at her son one minute, then shaking her hand the next? But she didn't want trouble, so she kept her thoughts to herself.

"You set off the silent alarm."

Sierra's heart skittered. "That's right. I forgot. Mrs. Drake told me I would need to disarm it. I'm so sorry, Officer." She offered the stocky blond man a tentative smile, wishing he'd leave. "I have the owner's phone number memorized. If you call her, she will clear this whole matter up."

"No need. I've already spoken with the security company monitoring the house."

"Good. You sure got here fast."

"I was nearby when the call came in. Are you and your son new to Sunriver?"

"In a way. I work for a local company, but before this we lived in Bend."

He nodded. "Welcome to the neighborhood. Most of the homes on this street are rentals." He pointed to a home three doors down and across the street. "Your closest full-time neighbor lives there. A retired couple."

"You seem to be well acquainted with this area."

He raised his chin. "Thank you. I try to make sure I know as many of the locals as possible."

"Does this mean you come around a lot?" her son asked with

a hint of annoyance in his voice.

She couldn't blame him, but she didn't allow sass. "Trey." The warning was all it took.

"Sorry. Excuse me." He marched past them and opened the back of the SUV.

Officer Preston frowned. "I guess I made a bad first impression on him. I'm sorry about that."

"It was an honest mistake and my own fault. I should have remembered to turn off the alarm."

"Will your husband be joining you, too?"

She narrowed her eyes. "Why do you ask?"

"Just like to know who is supposed to be here and who isn't." He raised a brow.

Irritation surged through her. This dude was seriously getting on her nerves. He didn't need to know her personal business. "No one else will be joining my son and me. Please excuse me." As the cop strode to his squad car, she walked over to her SUV and stacked one box onto another then strutted by the cop. *Whew!*

Spencer Preston stood at the water cooler in the bullpen at the police station, unable to get the pretty blonde who hadn't been wearing a wedding ring off his mind.

"Hey, Spencer. How'd it go today?" Mark, his buddy and fellow officer asked.

"Fine."

Mark crossed his arms and narrowed his eyes. "You are too easy to read. What happened?"

"Nothing."

Mark motioned for him to follow him into the conference room. "What's going on?"

Spencer ran a hand along the back of his neck. "I responded to a silent alarm call today. It turned out to be the house-sitter who forgot there was an alarm."

"And?"

Mark knew him too well. "And nothing." He didn't do anything wrong, but he couldn't shake that what happened today would be life altering.

"Nope." Mark shook his head. "I'm not buying what you're selling. Tell me."

"The woman intrigued me."

"How so? Is she someone we need to keep an eye on?"

"No. Nothing like that. I mean she snagged my interest." Except for one problem—her son. There was no way the teen would ever forgive him for what he did.

His buddy grinned. "Caught your eye, huh? I was beginning to think you were destined to remain single forever."

Spencer playfully slugged him in the gut. "Watch it. You've been here all of ten months. You don't know everything about me." Nor would he. There were some things he didn't talk about. Even with a good friend like Mark.

"Good point. Sorry. Catch you later." Mark sauntered to his desk and sat facing his computer.

Spencer was glad Mark didn't know his past. A churchgoer like him would likely only judge him. He'd judged himself enough and didn't need any help knowing what a fool he'd been. He waved to whomever might be paying attention as he left for the evening. It'd been a long day, and he was ready for the peace and quiet of his little house situated on the south side of Sunriver. It wasn't grand or glamorous, but it was affordable and close to work.

An image of the woman from the silent-alarm house flashed in his mind as he got into his pickup. Her fear-filled eyes heaped a load of guilt on him. He hated that he'd frightened Ms. Robbins and her son. She didn't look old enough to have a teenager. But he was smart enough to know people didn't always look their age, and some women had kids at a young age. Which one was she?

A sudden idea hit him and with renewed energy he headed to the Sunriver Village. He found exactly what he was looking for and purchased it. Who didn't love chocolate cake?

A short time later, he pulled into the driveway of the house he'd been called to this afternoon, grabbed the cake and got out. "Here goes nothing." The street looked as quiet as he'd expected. It wouldn't get busy until the weekend when tourists flocked to the resort community in droves to take part in winter activities on Mount Bachelor, which was less than a thirty-minute drive away.

He marched up the steps and rang the doorbell that gonged and seemed to echo. A moment later Sierra pulled the door open. "Officer Preston?"

He held out the chocolate cake. "I brought a peace offering. I felt bad about earlier, even if I was doing my job. That's no way to be welcomed to the neighborhood."

She hesitantly took the cake. "Thank you."

"Who is it, Mom?" Her son came up behind her and scowled when he spotted Spencer.

"Your local police officer bringing by a welcome-to-the-neighborhood cake." Spencer quirked a grin. Talk about sounding corny!

The kid frowned. Not the response he was hoping for.

Sierra stepped aside. "Trey, what do you say to Officer Preston?"

"Call me Spencer."

Trey's eyes narrowed. "Thanks, *Spencer*. For the record, my mom doesn't date."

"Trey!" Sierra's face reddened.

The teen shrugged. "What? You don't. And we both know he's only here because he either feels like a jerk for pulling a gun on me, or he's interested in you."

"That's enough."

Apparently Trey had a little sense in his head considering he took the cake and darted away.

"I apologize for my son. I'm afraid what happened this afternoon has had a lasting effect. He might need a few days . . . or months to get over it."

"I'm really sorry to hear that. I had no way of knowing you and your son weren't burglarizing the place. I wouldn't have been doing my job if I hadn't stopped him."

"Good point, and I'm thankful you weren't trigger happy." Spencer nodded.

A car pulled up behind his, and Bailey Calderwood, her boss, got out. "Hey there, Spencer. What's going on?" She strode up the stairs and stopped beside him.

He gave her the shortened version of what had happened and why he was there.

She shot a worried look at Sierra. "Are you okay?"

"I'm fine. What brings you by?"

"I wanted to see how your move went and if you needed anything."

"For the most part everything went well. That was really nice of you to stop in to check on us."

"I also brought you this." Bailey opened her purse and pulled out a paint wheel. "I've marked the colors I need you to order." She then pulled out two squares of fabric. "The homeowner decided to go with custom drapes and sheers. I'll leave that in your capable hands."

Spencer stood there silently taking in the women's conversation. Bailey was a friend of a friend. She managed the design side of Belafonte and Sons Construction and Design, a local interior decorating company that worked alongside the other branch of the company—new home construction. So Sierra must be the assistant he'd heard so much about. He should've put that together this afternoon.

"Do you want a slice, Spencer?" Bailey asked.

Both women stood there looking at him like he was a miscreant child.

"Why are you looking at me like I stole cookies from the cookie jar? What'd I miss?"

They both grinned and said in unison, "Nothing."

He took a step back. "O-kay. I'll be headed home then. Have a good evening, and I hope you enjoy the cake."

"We will," Bailey called after him as he retreated to his car.

He raised a hand and quickly got inside his pickup. He knew better than to daydream in the presence of two women. Too bad Bailey had stopped by. He'd really hoped to clear the air between himself, Sierra, and Trey.

He'd have to find another way to make this afternoon up to them. But how?

Releasing April 1, 2017

Books by Kimberly Rose Johnson

Sunriver Dreams
A Love to Treasure
A Christmas Homecoming

Wildflower B&B Romance Series
Island Refuge
Island Dreams
Island Christmas
Island Hope

Stand Alone
A Valentine for Kayla

Series with Heartsong Presents
The Christmas Promise
A Romance Rekindled
A Holiday Proposal
A Match for Meghan